SPECIAL MESSAGE TO READERS

THE ULVERSCROFT FOUNDATION
(registered UK charity number 264873)
was established in 1972 to provide funds for
research, diagnosis and treatment of eye diseases.
Examples of major projects funded by
the Ulverscroft Foundation are:-

- The Children's Eye Unit at Moorfields Eye Hospital, London
- The Ulverscroft Children's Eye Unit at Great Ormond Street Hospital for Sick Children
- Funding research into eye diseases and treatment at the Department of Ophthalmology, University of Leicester
- The Ulverscroft Vision Research Group, Institute of Child Health
- Twin operating theatres at the Western Ophthalmic Hospital, London
- The Chair of Ophthalmology at the Royal Australian College of Ophthalmologists

You can help further the work of the Foundation
by making a donation or leaving a legacy.
Every contribution is gratefully received. If you
would like to help support the Foundation or
require further information, please contact:

THE ULVERSCROFT FOUNDATION
The Green, Bradgate Road, Anstey
Leicester LE7 7FU, England
Tel: (0116) 236 4325

website: www.foundation.ulverscroft.com

THE HELLRAKERS

Meeting Van Connely and his gang is like coming face to face with hell . . . Skyler Lynch has hired the men, along with his friend Randy Staggs, to drive his horses southward to the Pocono country, where he and his daughter Kate have a ranch. But Connely steals the herd and murders Lynch before going on a rampage across the Southwest. Randy Staggs, left alive, vows to track him down, to the ends of the earth if necessary . . .

OWEN G. IRONS

THE HELLRAKERS

Complete and Unabridged

LINFORD
Leicester

First published in Great Britain in 2012 by
Robert Hale Limited
London

First Linford Edition
published 2013
by arrangement with
Robert Hale Limited
London

A catalogue record for this book is available
from the British Library.

ISBN 978–1–4448–1670–9

LP

Published by
F. A. Thorpe (Publishing)
Anstey, Leicestershire

Set by Words & Graphics Ltd.
Anstey, Leicestershire
Printed and bound in Great Britain by
T. J. International Ltd., Padstow, Cornwall

This book is printed on acid-free paper

1

Van Connely liked the Gilded Cage Saloon. It was pleasant and warm and it was raining coldly outside. He had a tumbler half filled with whiskey beside him. There was a plumpish girl in a pink silk dress sitting nearby, flashing her knees and a pleasant, if false, smile. It made no difference which; it was a part of her trade. Connely now turned his attention to his own trade which involved pasteboard cards, piles of chips and cash money. He had always enjoyed playing cards, even before he discovered that it was his natural profession. He liked the snap and gliding of them as they were dealt around the table. He liked peering at their undiscovered faces, calculating the odds and reading the eyes of his opponents. He enjoyed moving a pile of stacked chips into the center of the green baize table, watching for a small flinch on the other players' faces. Most of all he enjoyed raking in the wagered money and stacking it neatly at his elbow.

Of course, there were times that he lost, sometimes heavily, but this did not bother Van. The cards cannot always run right for you, and there would always be another day, a new deck dealt.

Just now as he sat watching the rain trickle down the windowpane beside him, watched as the yellow-haired saloon girl crossed her legs again, the Gilded Cage seemed one of the pleasantest places he had been in a long time. Shawnee Burns and Trapper McGee had come into Morrisburg with him, but these two were happily swilling whiskey and boasting or brawling at another night spot, the Dirty Shame, a rough-appearing establishment. Van Connely was in the mood for pleasant company and a little gambling.

The company wasn't that pleasant, but it did not matter. He found out as the evening rolled on that his fellow players included a sallow, haunted-looking man with a hooked nose, Jesse Sparks, who was the owner of the Gilded Cage; and the mayor of Morrisburg, a well-upholstered, self-satisfied looking man named Wayne Sevier. Although other players sat in from time to time, these two stayed at the table all evening. So did a man named Court Riddick who played cards as if he didn't understand the game. He had hairy hands and a single black eyebrow which sheltered his dark, brooding eyes like a caterpillar slithering across his frowning forehead.

The game now, with Jesse Sparks dealing, was five-card stud. Van Connely preferred playing draw poker where an individual player had the opportunity to discard when experience, the odds or simple intuition required it. With draw, especially five-card, you played the cards you were dealt. To Van it seemed to cut down on the skill of the game.

Just now, however, his hand was

looking good. He had an ace up, one hidden, and a pair of fours showing. He glanced at the faces of the other players. It might have appeared to them that he had only the pair of fours, or they might have been guessing that he had another one face down. Mayor Sevier who had a pair of tens showing might have had another; he bet like he did, and Jesse Sparks who had the six and seven of hearts showing might have been grooming a heart flush. Riddick, whose beetle brow showed only consternation, had a seemingly good pair of jacks up, but when he glanced at his hole cards his face grew dark.

The man was not designed for playing poker.

'Last card, boys — down and dirty,' Jesse Sparks said easily. He proceeded to deal around the table. His face was expressionless; he sucked at a tooth and drank a little more whiskey. Something about him bothered Van, but he would wait and see how the cards played out, then drift over and see how Trapper and

Shawnee were doing — or if the law had already picked them up.

Van's last blue-backed card skated across the table, face-down, and he lifted a corner of the card to have a peek at it. A third ace, which left him holding a full house, aces over fours. Not bad at all. Across the table Sparks was smiling thinly. Van was not smiling at all. The last card that had been dealt to him was the ace of diamonds. The problem was, so was his hole card.

'Bets? It's your bet, Riddick — those jacks of yours are the best showing.'

Riddick with incredible slowness looked at his hole cards and almost timidly shoved a ten-dollar gold piece into the center of the table. Mayor Sevier followed and bumped him twenty dollars. Jesse Sparks raised them an additional twenty.

'To you, Mister Connely,' Sparks said. Van studied his cards once again — *two* aces of diamonds. How was he to explain that when it came time to show his cards? He stared at Jesse

Sparks. Van hated a cheater. He especially hated a clumsy card sharp. Now if Van raised or even checked, his inexplicable ace would label him as a cheat himself, especially in Sparks's own saloon. There was no point in throwing good money after bad. Van carefully stacked his cards and announced:

'I'm out, boys. Thanks for the entertainment.'

Then, plugging on his hat which had rested on an empty chair beside him, leaving his earlier winnings on the table, Van went out into the cold of the rainy night, Jesse Sparks's hawkish eyes following him.

It was still raining, but it seemed a little lighter now. By keeping to the plankwalks in front of the town's buildings, all of which had awnings above them, he managed to stay mostly dry, except when he had to cross alleyways. Good thing — Van was wearing his freshly brushed and pressed pearl gray suit, his new boots and a yellow ascot. The boys had ribbed him before he left camp to come into Morrisburg, but Van had told them all that a man has to have his dignity, and outside of his honor, it was the most important thing he could possess.

Just now Van's dignity was taking a little roughing up. By the time he reached the Dirty Shame Saloon, his new boots were caked with mud, his suit damper than was comfortable despite his best efforts. Not that it mattered in a dive like the Dirty Shame. Filled with scoundrels and rough range-hands, local foul-mouthed drunks, no one could have cared how he was dressed.

There was a brief, violent uproar in the corner of the smoky room and Van Connely looked that way as a table was pitched over. He knew even before he came upon the scene — and sure enough, when he got to where the trouble was, he found Shawnee Burns, pistol in his hand, staring across the overturned table and scattered cards at a tough-looking bald man with a bushy mustache. Trapper McGee was braced against the wall, his hand empty, but resting near his own holstered Colt. Van decide to take charge.

'What's this, men!' he asked with a voice charged with false authority. 'You know we can't have any of this nonsense in here.'

The bald man and a couple of onlookers glanced at the man in the gray town suit, having no idea who he was, but believing he must be someone whose word counted for something around here. Not wanting to give the men time to question their first impression, Van continued:

'You three — straighten that table up; sit down and relax. You,' he said, leveling a finger at Shawnee Burns and at Trapper McGee, 'I want you to walk out of here now. No more trouble, do you understand me?'

'He called me a — ' Shawnee Burns objected reflexively. Van Connely cut him off.

'I said *now*, gentlemen. This sort of

activity can't be tolerated here.'

Grumbling something indistinct, Shawnee shoved his pistol into its holster, glared at the bald man and started toward the saloon door, Trapper McGee following while Van, seeming to shepherd them from the confines of the saloon out onto the dark rainy street, came last.

'Van!' Shawnee was complaining, 'I didn't need you to stop it. Why, if you knew what happened, what he called me — '

'Trapper?' he asked the taller of the two men.

'Ah, it was nothing, Van. Shawnee just decided he didn't like the man. Which, it seems to me,' he said to Shawnee, 'seems to happen every time you get past your third whiskey.'

'I notice you were ready to back him up,' Van said.

'I always will, but that doesn't mean I like his games.'

'All right. I understand that, but you two know how Captain Lynch frowns on these small incidents.'

9

'I've seen the captain . . . '

'That doesn't mean he would approve, does it? We'd better get our horses and travel back to the camp,' Van said. They could not see his thin smile in the darkness. 'After we take care of one little bit of business.'

Shawnee and Trapper followed Van silently to the stable where they had left their ponies. Van was not so concerned about the mud and the rain now, sloshing through it with a single purpose in mind. Retrieving their horses from the stableman, they saddled and mounted up. Van glanced at them — Shawnee still angry, but puzzled; Trapper McGee with his long hair falling to his shoulders. Trapper wore a hint of a beard, like someone had pressed an ink-stained thumb to his chin. Shawnee just wore his usual bristle of whiskers. It seemed that Shawnee never shaved but his beard never grew longer.

'Where's your rope, Trapper?' Van asked.

'Didn't bring one. Didn't see no need.'

'There's a need now — borrow that one,' he said, nodding at a coil of new hemp rope hanging on a nail on the stable wall.

Then they walked their horses out into the cold and blustery night. Van led them toward the Gilded Cage, explaining exactly what he had in mind. It made no sense to Shawnee or to Trapper, but Van was ramrod of the outfit, and what he said went. Besides, they deserved to have a little fun.

The Gilded Cage was bright and glittery through the curtain of rain. A woman — the girl in pink? — laughed. The voices inside were only murmurs against the sounds of the storm. Van could make out barely a word spoken inside the saloon as he swung down from his horse, lasso in hand.

There were three porch supports in front of the Gilded Cage, and each man looped his lasso around one of them. In the saddle, they tied hasty knots around

11

the pommels, and in unison backed their horses away into the muddy street.

When the ropes were taut, Van signaled with his hat and the horses backed again, with strength. The sound of cracking wood was loud even above the driving rain. The three supports broke almost in unison and the awning fell against the front of the building, shattering its windows, buckling a rafter. Inside voices cried out with urgency. People rushed toward the door, but there was no exit there with the fallen awning blocking the way. Van was carefully coiling his rope. He replaced it on its leather tie and nodded to his crew.

'All right, boys — that's all I had to say to them.'

*   *   *

The sky lightened as they rode the three miles toward the notch where the horses were kept, and by the time they had entered the narrow valley, the skies were clear enough to show clusters of silver stars between the parting clouds. It was cooler, but not uncomfortably so. They guided their horses toward the twin camp-fires burning low against the dark earth.

Van rode past a group of resting men seated around one of the low glowing fires and went directly to the chuck wagon. There he swung down. Before his boots had touched the ground, Captain Skyler Lynch had found him and he asked with some uneasiness:

'Did you manage to keep the boys out of trouble tonight, Van?'

'They were no problem, Captain.'

Skyler Lynch was not satisfied with the answer, but he saw no point in pursuing the matter further. Shawnee Burns had never been near a bottle of whiskey without something happening, and Trapper McGee was his best, perhaps only, friend and ally. However, Van had brought them back, intact and apparently sober. Lynch had other matters to worry about . . .

Specifically forty-four horses. No, he thought, make that forty-two. Two of them had wandered off the day before or had been taken by the Indians.

They were already short on men to drive such a large herd, one reason Lynch had been reluctant to let Trapper and Shawnee Burns go into Morrisburg. But the men were due a little relaxation after the long trail from Wyoming; besides he had sent Van Connely along to watch out for them.

The horse herd was not huge, but Skyler had invested almost all he had in them. Driving them south to Arizona from Wyoming where he had purchased them was a huge risk, but he had no other options left. His own ranch was dying after three years of drought. Horses were going for a good price in the southern lands. He figured that if all went right he could make enough out of the drive to save his ranch, keep his head above water for at least another year when, hopefully, the weather would return to its normal pattern and rain would again fall on his depleted grassland.

All of this was constantly in Skyler Lynch's mind as the herd made its way south. It was a gamble and he was undermanned. He had only seven riders, not counting himself — and that was the main reason he had been so reluctant to let any of them go into the nearby town for drinks and entertainment.

If Burns and Trapper McGee, for example, had been arrested on some charge and held in the Morrisburg jail to await trial, Lynch could not hold up the herd to wait for them. Tonight's rain was only a sample of what was to come if they did not quickly move the horses south. It was the time of year for hard rains followed by heavy snowfall. If his crew could handle the horses if they encountered bad weather, he could not say — they were having enough of a tough time now, undermanned as they were.

Even now, the half-wild horses, their

backs glistening in the starlight which shone through the broken clouds, looked restless, ready to run in all directions at the slightest provocation. They were much harder to handle on the trail than cattle, chiefly Skyler thought, because they were smarter — and swifter. Oh, horses were herd animals, too, but they were more likely to break from the group and take off on their own. True, a good cow pony could baffle a steer and pinch him back into the herd, but if one of these mustangs broke free, you had an out-and-out horse race on your hands.

Randy Staggs was approaching the tailgate of the wagon, leading his hammer-headed buckskin horse. Both looked miserable. It had been a long trail, and the rain had done nothing to improve anyone's spirits.

'Any coffee up, Captain?' Staggs asked.

'Over there,' Skyler Lynch said, nodding toward a low-burning fire.

'How are the boys doing?' Lynch asked with a touch of weariness.

16

'Not too bad,' Staggs answered as he crouched beside the tiny fire to hook the blue enamel coffee pot out. 'The box canyon is doing a good enough job of holding the horses although we've had a couple of 'em attempt to break out.' He rose to his feet, cup in hand to study the long, mustached face of Skyler Lynch. There was a tiredness in his eyes deeper than that caused by riding the long trail. Staggs looked briefly toward the skies which were mostly clear; only a few ragged, wind-driven clouds sheltered the stars from view.

'The boys could use some relief, Captain — they've been out there a long time now.'

'Yes, I know,' Lynch said heavily. 'I'll send Trapper, Shawnee, and Van Connely out after they've had a few minutes to rest.'

'All right — are they in shape for it?'

'Shawnee seems to have had a few too many drinks, but they should be all right.'

'As you say, Captain,' Randy Staggs replied doubtfully, touching two fingers to his hat brim.

Lynch nodded, watched as Staggs emptied his cup, tossed the dregs into the fire to hiss and strode away, leading his buckskin. All of the men had begun to call Lynch 'Captain,' although only Randy Staggs who had actually ridden with Lynch when he was a captain with the Texas Rangers had any reason to do so.

After his retirement Lynch had proved up on a hardscrabble parcel of eighty acres down in the Pocono country. He had left his daughter alone back there as a hostage to the elements and risked all he had on driving these horses through from Happy Forester's Wyoming ranch. If he succeeded he and Kate would be set up comfortably for many years to come. If he failed it would mean the end of all of his ambitions, all of his dreams.

At eighteen, Kate was a bold, cheerful girl — people said she was certainly her father's daughter — but she was unused to the deprivations of frontier life. At times Lynch regretted having brought her West, but she had insisted. After her mother's passing she had nowhere else to go.

Men were grumbling at each other now across the campsite. No doubt Randy Staggs had told them that they had a shift to ride this night. Walking across the muddy earth, collar pulled up against the chill of the night, Skyler Lynch started that way.

He wished he had a steady, experienced crew, but there were few around willing to ride eight hundred miles with him. After trying all the neighboring ranches in the Pocono Valley he had given it up and virtually raked hell to find the men who rode with him now. Van Connely — who might have been on the run from the law and considered himself a gambler and not a ranchhand; Shawnee Burns who was a drunkard on a downward spiral; and Trapper McGee who was overly fond of guns. These were the worst of them, and some of the others were not much better.

He was lucky to have run across Randy Staggs when he had — a trustworthy fighting man who had ridden many border trails with Lynch when they were both Rangers; the captain trusted and liked him.

There had been little trouble on the trail north. The weather held fair and the road was easily traveled. It was only when they started south again, pushing the herd of horses, that it seemed to dawn on the men that they were actually going to have to work for their pay.

'Just give me a little while to get my head together,' Lynch could now hear Shawnee Burns complaining. He saw Shawnee sitting up in his blankets, holding his head with both hands, Randy Staggs standing over him with no sympathy in his expression.

Lynch shook his head and started in that direction as the grumbling men were prodded to life. Was it going to be another five hundred miles of this? he wondered bitterly.

It was at that moment that they heard the sound of running horses approaching the camp, and in another minute the gun-toting riders burst out of the underbrush to confront them.

2

If no one else recognized the night riders, Van Connely did. Two of them at least. He had spent the evening sitting across a poker table from the saloon keeper, Jesse Sparks and Court Riddick, who looked more in his element here than he had playing cards. The big man's elongated single eyebrow was knotted above menacing eyes. He held his Colt steadily in his meaty hand. The third man was little more than a kid, his eyes wide with surprise as if he had not really expected to find the men they were chasing.

'We're looking for somebody,' the sallow saloon owner said, leaning forward over his horse's withers.

'We had that figured,' Randy Staggs said, stepping away from their horses a bit.

'Are you in charge here?' Sparks

wanted to know.

'I am,' Skyler Lynch said, stepping forward from the shadows to stand near Staggs. 'My name's Lynch. Who are you and what do you want here?'

Glancing to his right he saw that Shawnee Burns, Trapper McGee, and Van Connely had all gathered, standing near their beds. Each had a holstered gun belted on. Shawnee looked almost eager for trouble. Gunplay was one of his favorite forms of entertainment.

'Suppose you tell me what this is all about,' Skyler said in a neutral tone of voice.

Jesse Sparks sputtered a little as he answered. 'Three men wrecked my saloon! I don't know how long — or how much — it will take to repair the damage they did.'

'Do you know their names, what they look like?' Skyler asked reasonably.

'Just one of them. He was a sore loser in a poker game and came back with the other two, and they — '

'How do you know that's what happened?' Skyler asked. Staggs glanced at the captain and read enough to tell from his eyes that he was growing angry — not at the townsmen but at Trapper, Shawnee, and Van Connely, because there could be little doubt that they were the ones who had wrecked the saloon. Not that Skyler had any intention of turning them over to Jesse Sparks; they were short-handed as it was. The captain didn't wish to leave the three of them in the Morrisburg jail when he needed them so badly on the trail.

'All of my men are here and accounted for,' Skyler Lynch said. 'Unless you can identify them with certainty.'

'I told you I never saw but the one, blast you!' Jesse Sparks fired back, and as Randy Staggs watched, the captain's eyes narrowed, growing colder.

'What about that narrow *hombre*?' Court Riddick asked, jabbing a stubby finger in Van Connely's direction. Van had taken off his town suit and dressed again in his rough range clothes, and the twisting, smoky light cast by the low-burning camp-fires was nothing like the clear white light in the saloon. Jesse Sparks stared at Van Connely for a long time, perhaps trying to form an accusing, harsh glare to break the man. But Van Connely had a long trail behind him — he had lied to judges on the witness stand and laughed off the accusations of professional lawmen. Sparks's probing stare prompted no expression.

'Will you at least wait until morning when I can bring the marshal back here?' Sparks appealed to Skyler Lynch.

'I will not,' Lynch said firmly. 'I have a business to run, a herd of horses I need to deliver to home range. Make an arrest or make an identification now, or be damned with you.' Lynch said it calmly and quietly, but no man there doubted his determination.

'Told you we should have gathered up a posse,' the kid said, speaking for the first time.

'Shut up,' Sparks said roughly, his eyes still on the camping men. There were five of them to their three — if you could count Billy Slater, which Sparks did not. And if they were holding a herd of horses up the canyon, there would be at least that many more armed men around.

'We're going, but we'll be back!' Jesse Sparks vowed.

He was glaring suspiciously at Van Connely as he spoke, but Van only shrugged and set about rolling up his bed. With a last furious glance at the implacable Skyler Lynch and a muffled curse, Jesse Sparks yanked his pony's head around and started toward Morrisburg, the other two riders following him.

'I think he is mad enough to come back,' Randy Staggs said.

'I'm afraid I have to agree with you,' the captain answered with a touch of weariness. Then, 'All right, roll up the camp. We're going to drive the horses tonight.'

Staggs was expecting the order, but still was disappointed when he heard it. Driving a herd of half-broken horses across unfamiliar ground with an exhausted crew was not an enviable task. If they didn't lose a number of horses, they might well lose a number of weary men who figured they were being used unfairly. None of them were riding with Lynch out of a sense of loyalty to the brand. They were here for the job, and like any job it could quickly become untenable. The men that Skyler had hired out of necessity were, for the most part, roughnecks, bar-brawlers and small-time crooks — all used to making a living in easier ways. Randy Staggs had the idea that there were probably posters out on a few of them; that was why they had agreed to ride north in the relative safety of the drovers.

'We might have some quitters,' Staggs pointed out unnecessarily.

'We've known that from the start, Randy. There's nothing to be done about it. I collected most of them from under rocks and out of the gutters — let them go back there if they choose.'

There was extreme bitterness in the captain's words, but also resignation and determination. Three of his men had already disappointed him, and they were still hundreds of miles away from home.

It was bound to happen, Skyler reflected, would probably happen again, but he could only continue to try. For himself — and for Kate. He looked up at the sound of approaching boot steps. Van Connely was sauntering toward him across the dark campground, saddle in hand.

'Well, Van, what is it?'

'Me and the boys just wanted to thank you for standing up for us against those townies,' the sharp-eyed gambler said.

Skyler Lynch trembled briefly as if he had been struck by a cold gust of air. Connely may or may not have guessed that Lynch was trying to hold back his temper. The captain only said: 'Get off to work. Tell the others that there won't be any relief on this night. If they ask why — tell them.'

Not that Van Connely would — Skyler Lynch knew his men that well. Connely was unlikely to tell the men that he, himself, was the cause of their missing rest. He smiled thinly and strode away followed by the shuffling Shawnee Burns and Trapper McGee. With a deep sigh and a mingled curse and prayer Skyler went off to wake the cook and to catch up his own horse. It was going to be a long miserable night.

By the time Connely, Shawnee Burns, and Trapper McGee reached the canyon where the horses were being held, the men standing watch were seething.

'About time you showed up!' the black-bearded man called Tioga growled.

'No choice,' Van Connely said smoothly as his gray horse side-stepped uneasily in the mud beneath him. The ragged clouds skated past forming a sheer veil across the stars. The bearded Tioga sat his pony, waiting. There was a cold wind rising.

'The captain, he had us wait around until he made up his mind — him and Randy Staggs.'

'Made up their minds? About what?' Tioga asked with dull impatience.

'About what he was going to do — what we were to report to you,' Connely said as two other riders approached to join the conference: Shell Bodine and Slater.

'Well, are we finished here? I'm beat,' Slater said. Archie Slater had deeply sunk black eyes and a neatly trimmed black mustache. He didn't seem the kind of man to volunteer for drover's work, but probably like the rest of them he had been broke and desperate when approached by Skyler, perhaps eager to put miles between himself and the Pocono. For Slater had that definite, undisguisable look of a man with trouble on his back road. Slater never

30

confided in Connely as to what it was, but Van had the idea that they were two of a kind in background and spirit.

'Afraid not,' Van Connely told them. 'It seems that the captain has decided that we're going to drive the horses overnight.'

'What!' Tioga asked in angry disbelief. 'Why in hell would he do that? Half-wild broncos in the dead of night!'

'He doesn't explain things to me,' Connely said with an apologetic glance, which took in Tioga, Archie Slater and Shell Bodine, measuring their angry reluctance to follow the orders. Van shrugged. 'I don't mean to question his orders, but it makes no sense to me. If it were up to me . . . ' He let his voice fall silent meaningfully. Shrugging, he said, 'We've got no choice, boys — let's get them started as best we can.' He had made no mention of the angry Morrisburg townspeople, of course, and so the captain's order seemed either whimsical or bull-headed.

'The hell with this,' Tioga muttered

darkly. 'This is not what I signed on for — pushing broncos in the cold and dark with all this mud underfoot.'

'We'd better do the best we can,' Van said sympathetically. 'Maybe we will get extra wages for this.'

'We might take a lot more than that out of this,' Slater responded which was just the sort of reaction Van Connely had been fishing for.

The horses were roused, bunched and started southward. The animals were in a fractious mood; they had two attempts at a break-out before they had even reached the mouth of the canyon. The men grumbled, swore, and pushed on. That was the state of matters when Randy Staggs reached the herd. He rode his buckskin up beside Van Connely and spoke:

'Did you explain to them, about the townsmen possibly riding after us?'

'I explained it as best I could,' Van Connely said innocently. 'They still don't like it.'

'No,' Staggs replied, 'I didn't expect

them to — uh, oh — look at that palomino; he doesn't want to go along!'

Randy heeled his horse after the break-away wild horse, leaving Van Connely behind. Van smiled thinly, and rode steadily, silently on through the night until Shawnee Burns caught up with him.

'What are you up to, Van? Is it what I think?'

'You know me well enough.'

'Yes, I suppose I do,' Shawnee agreed.

'What do you think the herd will bring — cash money? I'm thinking something like three thousand dollars.'

'More. With any luck, four or five thousand. Depending on how many horses we get through with. It's going to be a long drive.'

'We sell them at the first chance we have — by then we'll have lost any posse those Morrisburg jackasses can raise,' Van believed.

'If we get half that amount, we'll be better off than we are working for ranch-hand wages. But what about the captain — and Staggs? We have to assume Randy Staggs will stand by the old man, being his old Ranger buddy.'

'You can count, can't you, Shawnee.'

Burns blinked and scowled before he responded. 'I guess I can, well enough. You're saying that there's only the two of them against the rest of us if the other boys stand with us.'

'I think they will. None of them were cut out to be cowboys either.' Van leaned back in the saddle looking briefly skyward. 'You know, Shawnee, my friend, that's the one problem with hiring crooks to work for you: you've got a bunch of crooks working for you.' Van smiled and then straightened in the saddle as a blue roan, aggravated by the loss of sleep, the cold, the mud underfoot, and its human masters' unreasonableness broke free of the herd.

'Let's get him, Shawnee!' Van Connely said. 'From here on we're working for ourselves and every pony we lose is cost-ing us money.'

* * *

After midnight it began to rain again. Skyler Lynch had given the cook, Angelo, a hand hitching the team to the chuck wagon. Now they turned the herd southward, riding on relentlessly with the stiffening wind at their backs, gusting strongly enough so that it seemed to threaten to knock a man out of his saddle. The rain, which had began to fall gently from the thin clouds, now fell heavily as a reinforcing storm arrived from the north with tumultuous fury. Skyler Lynch rode close to the herd both to keep them closely bunched, and because their massed bodies threw off heat.

The night turned black and bitter. Randy Staggs kept his buckskin horse close to the flank of the herd, closer than he would have dared with horned steers. Glancing back he could see no one, only the backs and glittering eyes of the unhappy horses. The wind was fitful, the rain constant, the temperature dropping precipitously. Hunched in his waist-length leather coat, Staggs trembled with each icy blast that swept across the prairie. Using his coiled riata, he kept nudging the horses into a tighter bunch. They plodded on, shoulder to shoulder, not liking the restriction much.

Randy's nemesis was a devil-eyed black stallion with a blaze on its nose and one white stocking on its right front leg. The HF-connected brand it wore was like a fresh scar on its flank. The animal was in a miserable temper, it seemed, and decided to take its mood out on Randy Staggs. The horse would bolt toward the perimeter then lose itself among the herd. Then it would make its way again to the fringe and appear ready to bolt, only to turn back again, its eyes fixed challengingly on Randy as if daring this man-thing to try to tame it.

The horses were forced to slow and come to a stop at a deep coulee slashed across the plains. Lightning flashed, and by its illumination Randy saw that there was only one way across — straight down a sandy bluff, which ended at a fast-flowing rivulet, then straight up the farther bank.

He could not remember passing this way on their ride north, but probably they had veered far off the trail under these conditions. They were not going to have the time to look up- and downstream from there for a better crossing. Not with the restive, milling horses ready to bolt at any moment. Besides, he was thinking, they likely had a posse from Morrisburg on their heels by now. These, if they were coming, would not be slowed by having to tend the balky herd. They would be riding flat out across the plains, blood in their eyes.

Lightning struck again, very close this time, sending an electric glow across the empty land, disturbing the wild horses even more. Randy glanced beside him and saw the captain approaching him, shoulders hunched beneath his sheepskin coat.

'What do you think, Randy?' Skyler Lynch called above the pitch and whine of the wind.

Staggs expelled his breath through tightly pinched lips and shook his head. 'There's no choice, I don't think, Captain. We've got to push them across here or camp again.' And they couldn't make camp again — it was pointless.

'I suppose you're right,' Skyler said heavily. His face looked weighted down by the years. His eyes could not be seen in the darkness of night. 'What I'd give for a crew of good Texas cowboys!' he exclaimed. Randy knew what he meant; a crew of experienced hands would have a tough job of it, driving the horses into the gully and out again, but they would get the job done. With the rag-tag crew the captain had assembled for this drive, it seemed a nearly impossible task.

'There's no choice, Captain,' Randy said.

'No, there isn't. We're going across — pass the word, would you, Randy?'

Randy Staggs set out to circle the horse. The rain drove down. It stung his eyes and soaked through his jacket, adding the cold weight of water to his shoulders. Once Randy thought he felt the colder kiss of snow against his cheek. He found Van Connely and Shawnee Burns sitting their horses side by side and gave them the orders to push on into the coulee. Connely only nodded — the man seldom showed expression. Burns grumbled something indistinguishable and reached into his saddle-bags where he carried a smuggled bottle of whiskey. What was Randy to do, scold him? He started on to find the other men giving them the best instructions he could.

These, however well-intentioned and considered, were not going to be easy to follow in this weather with the horses plunging down to the river bottom against their will. 'Try to keep them bunched in the coulee bottom. When we push them up on the other side, we'll have to pinch them off at the head so they won't run out onto the plains,' he said in variations to Trapper McGee, Tioga, and Shell Bodine.

'Do you want to talk to Angelo yourself?' Randy asked when he again found Skyler Lynch.

'I suppose so,' the captain said wearily. 'We'll have to cut his wagon loose, you know?'

'I know it — though you could let him follow the coulee along eastward, seek out an easier crossing . . . if one exists.'

'I'll give Angelo the option,' Skyler said. 'I haven't done so well at making decisions so far.'

'Captain . . . ' Randy began sympathetically, reaching out to touch his shoulder, but before he could continue there were three sharp reports and Randy saw Skyler go suddenly erect in his saddle, hand clasped to his chest.

Then Randy felt his buckskin horse's front knees buckle and give way and he was thrown over its neck to the cold, dark earth as dozens of wild horses dashed past his head and plunged into the coulee.

He must have been knocked out as he fell, because as Randy tried to grope his way up to full consciousness, his head whirled and his limbs seemed disconnected from his body. There was thick mud beneath him, a driving mesh of cold rain surrounding him. The night offered no visibility. A soft nearby moan caused Randy to grope around with his hands like a blind man in the night, and his fingers touched the captain's shoulder.

Skyler Lynch reached out and gripped Randy's wrist.

'Thank God!' the captain said hoarsely. 'I thought I was all alone. Who is it? Is that you, Randy?'

'Yes, sir.'

'I knew I could count on you. I always could. I'm hit pretty bad,' he said, his voice weakening.

'You've been hit before — and survived,' Randy said, sitting up with crossed legs beside the wounded man. The snow, now, was beginning in earnest. Large flakes were falling across Skyler's face and the injured man did nothing to brush them off.

'I'm afraid this is worse,' Skyler said, and he coughed once, violently, so that crimson blood trickled from the corner of his mouth. 'It must have been the posse, don't you think, Randy? I mean such as they are, my own men wouldn't do this, would they?'

'No, sir. I'm sure not,' Randy lied.

'The horses . . . ?'

'They've crossed the coulee,' Randy said reassuringly. Skyler's hand fell away from Randy's then.

'But you stayed with me?' Skyler Lynch said.

'Sure, Captain,' Randy Staggs answered, not telling the old Ranger that he had had no choice about it.

'You're a good man, Randy,' Skyler

said. 'You'll see to my daughter, won't you? Make sure Kate gets her share.'

'You won't need me to see to that — a little rest and you'll be fine,' Randy said, shivering in his jacket as the wind twisted snow over them.

'I don't . . . if I . . . ' Skyler began, stumbling over his words. He was silent for a long while as the wind whipped past, crackling as it rumbled through the dry willow brush in the coulee beyond. 'Randy!' Skyler said with sudden urgency.

'Take off my boot — my right one.'

'I don't — '

'Do it!' Skyler insisted and Randy struggled to his knees to see to the odd request. The wind pummeled his back, drifting fresh snow over the captain's face. Two tugs and he had the captain's old cavalry boot removed.

'Feel around inside, Randy. That lump along the seam. Do you have your knife? Slit it open,' he ordered through chattering teeth. Randy Staggs complied. Taking his Bowie knife from its sheath at the back of his belt he opened the lining of the boot with its tip. Something tumbled free. Turning the boot upside down he shook the contents out. Ten twenty-dollar gold pieces fell into his palm.

'Got 'em?'

'Yes, sir.'

'Happy Forester cut me a good deal on the horses — for old times' sake.' Skyler coughed again, again producing blood. 'The bill of sale is in my coat pocket — take that, too.' With his eyes closed now, he lay his head back against the cold, dark earth. 'It's all I have left in the world, Randy. See that Kate at least gets that money. It will buy her train fare East. I don't want the girl to have to . . . '

Randy remained seated beside Skyler, waiting for him to continue even though he knew Skyler would not. The captain had fought his last battle, against an opponent no man can defeat. He couldn't have said how much longer he sat there, but as the snow deepened and the wind increased across the blackened plains, he knew that he had to rise or they would discover his body lying there beside the captain's. He rose to his feet with painful stiffness and faced away from the wind. Then, after salvaging what belongings he could, he staggered ahead on foot across the raw land in the stormy night, leaving the dead behind, his enemies far distant, secure and seemingly safe from retribution.

3

The cold fury of the storm continued unabated. Lowering his eyes to avoid the blasts of the freezing wind, Randy Staggs made his way toward the edge of the coulee. His hope was to avoid some of the wind by clambering down into its depths. Close beside one of the bluffs, he might be sheltered from the frigid gusts. Descending was no easy task. The bluff was nearly sheer, the ground underfoot a mixture of snow patches and loose sand. The small rill he had seen earlier had become a rushing, bitterly cold creek showing white water as it drove over exposed tree roots and rocks.

Along the river bottom Staggs could still see signs of the stolen herd's passing. Memories of Skyler Lynch's lost dream.

The snowstorm pelted his face as he

peered north, and so he turned southward, putting the wind at his back and trod on, searching for a place to shelter for the night. The darkness was nearly complete. Only the snow appeared white; the rest of the world had sunk into blackness. Randy Staggs plodded on — across ground that was muddy, snow-crusted and featureless.

Half a mile on he found what he was looking for. Thirty feet or so up along the bluff there was a dark hole through the general white blanket now draped across flanks of the coulee. A cave seemed to have formed itself around the roots of a fallen sycamore tree. The tree lay sprawled against the earth like a felled soldier in the war against the elements. Staggs started that way. Slipping, sliding, crawling on hands and knees, Randy made his way towards it.

It wasn't much in the way of shelter. The hollow, still partially screened by the dead sycamore's root system was no more than six feet deep, less than that in height. Randy dragged himself into the small opening and was immediately grateful that he had found the shelter. The moaning whip of the gusting wind was cut off. The earth was clear of ice, free of mud. Dropping the few items he carried, he sat, knees drawn up, and stared out at the turbulent night. The wind outside drove the constant snow; the creek tumbled and roared in its passing.

What now? For warmth he had his buckskin horse's saddle-blanket and Skyler Lynch's sheepskin coat, which he had reluctantly stripped off the dead man. Perhaps that was enough for him to survive the night. If the storm settled in for days, he would likely freeze to death in time.

All right! First things first. He had to survive this night and hope for a brighter morning. Again he unsheathed his bowie knife from where it rode on the back of his belt, and on his knees began to work at the dead roots of the blown-down tree. These were surprisingly dry, having been sheltered by the cave from rain and snow. And Randy cut them into useable lengths, forming a small cone of twigs near the mouth of the cave; bunches of small dead roots were manufactured into tinder. Then, leaning back on his heels, Randy took the small stainless-steel cylinder containing his matches from his jacket pocket and tried to strike flame to the tiny camp-fire.

It took three matches. The wind seemed to stretch cold frustrating fingers into the cave to thwart his efforts. Finally though, a clump of bark and bare root caught the tiny flame of the match and sputtered into smoky, fiery life. The small fire grew and cast smoky shadows across the interior of the cave. Randy set about making his bed, such as it was.

He considered his situation and pointed his feet toward the fire, his head away. The smoke otherwise would be drifting across his face, and there was the odd chance that his hair might catch fire. Besides, at the moment, his feet seemed by far the coldest part of his body. Making the best of what he had to cover himself, Randy curled up tightly beneath his blankets and tried to sleep as the cold wind drove swirling snow past the mouth of the cave. Smoke filled the tiny hollow and the cold intensified. His feet were temporarily warmer, but as for the rest of his body it trembled and shuddered and drew itself more tightly together beneath his thin covering. He lay, knees drawn up, gripping his arms tightly across his chest, teeth chattering, waiting for the blessed numbness of deep sleep.

★   ★   ★

It was warmer. Randy Staggs felt something heavy and comforting thrown over him. He knew by its feel and scent that it was a heavy buffalo robe, but in his half-waking state he did not bother to try to analyze how that could be. The night was bleak, black and cold, yet his fizzling camp-fire had been given fresh fuel. He knew that from the vivid red and yellow patterns on the wall of the cavern he glimpsed through one partially opened, quickly closed eye. Then the corner of the buffalo robe was drawn back and someone slipped in beside him. Randy did not move, did not try to see who it was.

But he knew by her scent and some deeper instinct that it was a woman. He was careful not to touch her, careful not to roll his head and look. She was a woman, and she had come to save him. He remained absolutely still as the robe and the near presence of her warmed him as the dreadful night swept past.

He slept in deep comfort until the first light of a brilliant new morning glared into the cave. Randy lifted his head, seeing the sun, blue-white and harsh glinting across the snowfields, sparkling on the face of the river below.

Someone was yelling up at them and he got to his knees to squint out against the brilliance of the morning. Three men sat their ponies below. They were Cheyenne Indians. And they appeared angry. Two of them carried lances; the other, the young brave riding a paint pony, had only a bow and quiver of arrows. He was the one doing the shouting, and as Randy leaned back, his hand resting on his holstered Colt, the young woman who had come to him in the night, rose, picked up her buffalo robe and walked past him, bent half-over. She wrapped the robe around her as she emerged and strode toward the waiting men with regal strides, like a summoned princess.

Randy did not dare to move as she reached the three men on the bank of the river. The young warrior on the paint pony called out to her three more times in a demanding voice, saying something that sounded like, 'Hathet yo!' but the princess ignored his command, if that was what it was, and simply walked to his horse and swung up behind the youth. Then, without so much as a backward glance at Randy

Staggs, the group rode away to the north, leaving Randy deeply puzzled but deeply relieved.

'I'll be damned,' he muttered as the three horses rounded a bend in the coulee bottom and disappeared into the northlands.

He gave the matter only a few minutes of speculation — there were more important matters to be considered.

There was a band of cold-blooded killers with a herd of stolen horses loose on the plains, and they were his responsibility. A band of men who had brought trouble down upon the captain and then stolen his horse herd — Lynch's last hope for a decent life in retirement — and for his daughter to forge a good life with. They had killed Skyler Lynch and left the old Texas Ranger to die in the snow. They would drink up the profits or throw their money away on gambling tables without regret. Never giving a thought to the hard-working men and good women

53

they were harming.

Randy Staggs had already decided that it was his job to find them — each and every man — and remind them of it.

First there was a more immediate obligation to tend to. The captain's last request.

He had to somehow reach Arizona and find Lynch's ranch along the Pocono and deliver the gold he was holding to the captain's daughter. That could not wait. The girl doubtless had debts and needs to be taken care of. That had to be seen to first before he could even consider how to take up the long trail and administer justice to Van Connely and his gang of killers.

* * *

By mid-morning Randy Staggs had made his way across the raging stream and up the treacherous slope of the coulee. He had found the shattered remains of the chuck wagon in the gully. Most of its contents had been stripped, and there was no way he could carry much, but he did come across a tin of salt biscuits and a jar of honey, which he stuffed into his jacket pockets. It wasn't much, but he wasn't going to make it far without a thing to eat.

The prairie gleamed with white brilliance, like scattered diamonds. The reflection of the sun off the snow caused him to squint continuously as he plodded on. There was no sign of the passing horse herd — the snow had covered their tracks — and on the horizon no structure stood. Only endless miles of snowfield.

The faint snuffling sound caused Randy to halt in his tracks and look around. The black horse with the white blaze and stocking stood twenty yards off, staring at him. Being a herding animal it needed to be near other animals, Randy thought, and he happened to be the only animal on the wide empty prairie.

'Come along here, then,' Randy coaxed, crouching down and extending a hand. The horse just glared at him with its well-remembering, evil eyes. Randy tried again, even offering one of his biscuits to the horse. It came no closer, only shaking its head so that its mane swirled around its neck.

'To hell with you, then,' Randy said after long minutes. He could have used that horse, but it was a stubborn devil. He began again, one foot before the other, squinting into the glare as he trudged southward. He cursed Van Connely, Shawnee, and the rest of them as he walked. To leave a man out here afoot was the same as killing him. He stopped and turned abruptly. The horse was still there; no closer, no farther behind. Its eyes reflected intelligence and recalcitrance. 'You know, we could make a good pair,' Randy said, wasting more time with the animal. He approached the black but it spun on its hoofs and danced off a little way to stand glaring at him.

'To hell with you,' Randy muttered again in frustration. He could waste half a day trying to make friends with the lost horse with no success. He walked on, hearing the steady clop of the black horse's hoofs behind him. Wasn't there some fable about a stalking horse? Randy thought so, but could not bring it to mind. He realized he was only trying to focus his mind on something other than the cold, and the fiery wish for revenge that burned in his heart.

When exhaustion began to set in, he paused on a low knoll where a dead or winter-starved oak tree stood like wrought iron against the brilliant sky, sat on his blanket and dug two biscuits from his pockets, slathering them with honey from the jar. His hasty meal did little to assuage his hunger, but at least it filled some of the empty space in his stomach. His was going to be an Indian-style diet for some time now — eat as much as he could of whatever he could find at the time because he wouldn't know where his next meal might be coming from.

How far had he to go? There must be some sort of settlement he could reach before he starved to death or another blizzard swept across the plains. But in what direction? He had no idea; his head throbbed as he tried to form some sort of plan.

The black horse stood a little way off, watching him.

He was tired of cursing the animal, tired of trying to tame it. He rose heavily and started on — southward, as if he could escape the snows and the harsh winds if he could only slog farther south. As he walked he watched for any sign of men having passed across the snowfields — their direction might give him an idea of what course he should set for himself. But there was nothing: no footprints, wheel ruts, or horses' hoofs had marred the surface of the snowfield. He was the last man alive in a frozen world.

The day rolled by and his legs began

to stiffen as the slow miles passed. Worse, the sun was wheeling slowly westward coloring the blank sky. It was growing cooler and as night settled, the temperature would drop dangerously. Randy would find himself in the unsheltered open without even the feeble comfort of a camp-fire. And then they would find him — beneath the snow. He stumbled on desperately, searching the land for some sort of shelter — even as crude a one as he had spent the previous night in. There was nothing.

He paused, heard the stupid black horse whicker, and glanced that way. It stood, ears pricked, nostrils flaring, looking toward the west.

'What is it, you devil?' Randy murmured. Could it be that the horse smelled others of its kind, sensed salvation? Randy had no idea, but as the sky darkened, he decided that he might as well trust the horse's instincts as his own. He started toward the sunset sky, the black horse following him at a distance.

Half an hour on as the sun spread a last garish flush of color against the sky, Randy thought he saw something. Some sort of geometric form silhouetted against the dull crimson sky. He staggered on, and with each step the shape seemed to take on substance, to form itself into a building of some sort. And now there were other structures. Randy gasped with anticipation as he walked on, more strongly now, toward the tiny hamlet.

For that was what it was. He — they — had somehow managed to stumble upon a small ramshackle town on the long plains. Randy did not slow his pace; it seemed an urgent matter to march on as quickly as he could. It was a matter of survival.

Reaching the town limits Randy Staggs stood staring like a traveler coming upon a forbidden palace in the depths of a jungle. The slovenly town was that beautiful to him, more so perhaps. This town, announced by a crudely painted sign to be 'Blind Man's Springs', was a beacon of survival. Randy knew he would not have survived another night on the plains, and the tumbledown settlement of adobe and logs, rough planks and tin sheeting was like Mecca to him.

He stumbled along the street, wading through the half-frozen mud. He had to find food — and a bed! But where? The first light he saw lit was in a two-storey building with gaping front doors. A stable, obviously, and he went that way. Passing through the double doors he felt the force of the cold wind abate. The light from a single lantern seemed bright enough to pierce his eyes. He could barely make out the shadow of a man as the stable-hand approached him.

'Look like you've had some trouble,' the man said kindly.

'Yes. I took the wrong road some-where,' Randy answered wearily. 'Look, I need something to eat and a place to

61

bed down. Any advice?'

'Mae — that is Mae Lincoln — has a small restaurant at the edge of town. It's not much to look at, but she can fry a steak and makes decent apple pies. She's also got a few rooms she lets out to travelers.'

'Sounds like what I'm looking for,' Randy said. 'I thank you.'

'Will there be anything else?' the tall, narrow stable-hand asked.

'I don't think so.'

'What about shelter for your horse?'

'My . . . ?' Puzzled, Randy turned around to find the evil-eyed black stallion standing in the double doors of the stable, looking angry and hopeful at once. Randy Staggs laughed. 'Might as well, I suppose. If you can handle him, bring him in and give him a rubdown and a bait of oats.'

The stable-hand scowled with injured pride. 'If I can't handle him, mister, he's no natural animal.'

Then as Randy watched in astonishment, the man walked to the door, wrapped his fingers in the horse's mane, ran a hand over his sleek flank and led it to a stall. 'This *is* your horse, ain't it?' the stable-hand asked as he backed the black horse into a stall.

'I suppose — I found it loose on the plains,' Randy said. He was now leaning against the stable wall, trying to save the little energy he had left. 'Not that he's much use to me.'

The stable-hand slapped the black's rump admiringly, 'Nice looking animal.' Walking toward Randy, his expression darkened. 'The reason I ask, friend, is that a while ago we had some men ride through here with horses sporting that same HF-connected brand and they made themselves unwelcome in no time.'

'I wouldn't know anything about that,' Randy said. 'As I told you, I found this horse wandering the plains. As far as I know, it's never been ridden — by me or anyone else,' he told the dubious man. 'Now, where did you say I could find this Mae's place?'

It was not until he had eaten and was wrapped snugly in bed beneath a low ceiling in one of Mae Lincoln's boarding house rooms with the tormenting wind periodically rattling his window that Randy Staggs realized he should have paid more attention to the stable-hand, asked a few questions about the men who had arrived in town with HF-connected horses and made themselves 'unwelcome'. It had to have been Van Connely, Shawnee, and the rest of the crew, driving the stolen horses toward some unknown destination.

But, Randy reflected, what good would it do him to know their direction of travel, if anyone knew it? A lone man without even a horse trying to follow Van Connely's gang across the wild country was a reckless idea, and likely to prove fruitless if not deadly.

No, he thought, tugging the blankets up more tightly under his chin. The thing to do was to let them go for now and follow through with his promise to

Skyler Lynch: take the little bit of gold money left over from the buying of horses and deliver it to Kate Lynch. One of the twenty-dollar pieces he had already had to break to provide himself with food and lodging, but he thought that neither Skyler himself nor Kate could fault him for that.

He had met Kate only once, down on the Pocono after Skyler had recruited him to ride along on the trip to Happy Forester's distant ranch, and he had little memory of the girl. She had dark hair, was slender and large-eyed. They hadn't exchanged more than a dozen words, these the conventional pleasantries of meeting.

She would need the money soon enough, no doubt about that. Skyler had told Randy that he was investing everything he had in this last attempt to bring the Pocono ranch to profitability. A woman alone with no livestock would not last long on that poor ranch. She would be struggling just to buy food, if she was not already doing so. Seeing to her needs was more important than chasing madly after the murderer, Van Connely and his gang. He would have to let them go on their way.

For now.

4

The light shining through the window of Randy Staggs's window was clear and bright. The glass seemed nearly blue with its illumination. He opened his eyes to watch dust motes swirling across the room, tiny golden flecks. Sitting up, he reached first for his hat — an old Western custom — then for his jeans which he slid into with only an occasional complaint from his travel-weary legs. Boots and shirt were drawn on next, and he walked to the window to stare out at the slovenly little prairie town. Beyond it he could see melting snow, now showing patches of brown earth here and there as the morning sun touched it.

He frowned as he considered his situation — he still had no idea of how he could reach the Pocono. True, he could have spent more of Skyler's money buying a horse, but he was unwilling to chip more out of Kate's small inheritance. It was going to be hard enough to tell her that her father was dead, that this was all the money she had in the world. Taking in a deep, slow breath, Randy stepped out of the small room and walked toward the scent of coffee in the dining area beyond.

There were five men there already, finished with their breakfast and sipping coffee. Two of them were fur traders Randy had met briefly the night before who were waiting for the weather to clear. These two had shared one of the other rental rooms in the boarding house. He nodded to them and sat himself in the corner of the low-beamed room, observing as he waited for coffee to be brought to him.

Two of the other men were roughly dressed, obviously local people from the way they gibed with the waitress and with Mae Lincoln herself, who bustled about with a big blue-enamel coffee pot gripped with a kitchen towel. The matronly Mae served Randy and asked if his room had suited him, then bustled away toward the kitchen in the rear. More men were arriving, stamping their boots on the boardwalk outside to try removing the mud and slush from them. Greetings were exchanged all around as the local men met each other.

In a corner sat a stranger like Staggs. He wore tall fringed boots and had a pair of fringed gauntlets resting on a chair beside him. His hair was corn-yellow, his mustache long and tinged with gray. His eyes seemed to be watching everyone even though he kept them fixed on his coffee mug.

'Who's that?' Randy asked out of curiosity, nodding toward the man as Mae returned to top off his cup of coffee.

'Him?' She glanced that way. 'Don't know his name — one of the new line drivers, I think.'

'Stagecoach?'

'Yup,' Mae said with evident pride. 'We've finally gotten big enough that they run through here — every Wednesday and Friday.' She hurried away again. Randy rose with his coffee cup and made his way across the room. As the stagecoach driver looked up, Randy nodded and took a chair.

'Mind if I sit down here?'

'Help yourself. What can I do for you?' the keen-eyed stage driver asked.

'I'm trying to make my way back to the Pocono country. I was wondering if your route takes you that way.'

'End of the line is at Colton. Do you know where that is?'

'Roughly. I know it's nearer to where I'm going than here.' Randy smiled.

'I can't sell you a ticket,' the driver said. 'I believe they do that over at the general store.'

'I'm not sure I could afford one,' Randy said.

'Down and out, are you?' the mustached man asked with a frown.

'The next thing to it,' Randy admitted.

'I see. That's always tough — especially out here.' He sat thoughtfully appraising Randy for a long time before he asked, 'Have you got any army experience?'

'No. I was with the Texas Rangers for two years, though.'

'Even better,' the driver said, resting his forearms on the table as he leaned forward. 'I thought you had that sort of look about you. Look, mister, I've been sitting here since dawn waiting for my helper to show up. He might've got caught in the storm. I'll let you go along to Colton — if you're willing to ride shotgun. There's been some trouble down in the Gower Hills and I could use someone. What do you say?'

'I'd say this is my lucky morning,' Randy said sincerely. He introduced himself and the driver took his hand.

'I'm Barry Hampton. How soon can you be ready to leave, Randy?'

'How about now?'

The driver glanced at his pocket watch. 'I've just got to give any last-minute passengers another five minutes. Then we're on our way.'

There were no last-minute passengers. In fact there were none at all waiting at the coach which sat behind the stable. Randy could see the red-painted coach with its yellow wheels through a small back door, see the rumps of a bay horse. He looked around, motioning to Hampton.

'One minute,' he said, and the stage driver went out to check his rig. Randy found the stable-hand in a back office. There he paid for the black's feed of the night before.

'You're riding on the stage?' the man asked in puzzlement.

'That's right.'

'Well . . . what do you want me to do about your horse?'

'Keep it, sell it if you can. I don't care.'

'You can't just leave your horse!'

'I have to — I don't care what you do

with it. It's no use to me — I can't ride it, can't eat it, and anyway it isn't mine,' Randy said. He said it with conviction, but when he walked out into the stable area, there was that black devil, its head over the stall, eyeing him with that same evil glance. The eyes reflected something else, Randy thought — disappointment? It's stupid to ascribe human emotions to animals, besides, Randy had to be going, and what he had said to the stable-hand was true.

Behind the building someone whistled shrilly — Barry Hampton had a schedule to meet, and he was eager to be rolling.

The land was damp, raw, and cold with snow covering the earth in the hollows and the shadows. Ahead the barren, cactus-stippled form of the layered Gower Hills stood like low sentries against a pale morning sky. That way, Randy Staggs knew, lay Colton, a small but prospering town not that far from the Pocono country. If he could reach Colton, he was sure he could find a way to reach the Lynch ranch and give Kate Lynch her father's last gift to her.

'What the hell's that?' Barry Hampton muttered. Randy saw that the stagecoach driver, always vigilant, was now glancing behind the swaying coach and Randy, too, looked that way, his hands tightening on the borrowed express gun he held.

'What do you see?' he asked Hampton.

'A horse, but it seems it's riderless.'

Randy narrowed his vision and as the coach rolled on, he could make out the animal running at speed. Following the stage. A black horse with a white blaze and one white stocking. Randy Staggs grumbled a curse.

'What is it?' Hampton, always on the lookout for trickery, asked. 'Whose horse is that?'

'I suppose it's mine,' Randy answered sourly. 'It must have broken out of its stall and decided to follow us along.'

'Your horse?' Hampton said, giving

Randy a dubious glance. 'Then why aren't you riding it?'

'We have never reached an understanding about that,' Randy replied. 'Don't give it a thought — it's bound to give it up after a while.'

Barry Hampton nodded and returned his concentration to guiding his team over the slushy land toward the forbidding landscape ahead. The driver said nothing, but Randy could guess at his thoughts. Hampton had begun this leg of his trip wary of robbers. Now with the unexplained horse appearing, he must have been wondering if it was not some thief's clever plan — rob the coach and have his well-trained horse at the ready to make his escape on.

As they reached the gray hills, Hampton was forced to slow the horses for the upgrade. Snow clung to every crevice in the rocks. Nopal cactus sprouted abundantly. Otherwise there was no flower, bush, or tree along the road. The horses labored up the road into the gap. The shadows of the bluffs fell chillingly over them as they climbed higher.

'I thought I saw sunlight on metal,' Barry Hampton huffed through his yellow mustache. 'Watch that patch of rocks to the south.'

Randy nodded silently and lifted the shotgun higher, cradling it in the crook of his arm, his eyes searching the indicated rock pile. He hoped that Hampton was mistaken. He had finally found a way to make his journey southward, finally gotten himself fed and rested. He wished for nothing less than a gunfight.

But as Barry guided the team past the rocks and began to take the bend in the trail beyond, two men popped up. One behind them, appearing like a shadow from the stacked rocks, the other directly in front of the coach, legs spread, rifle at his shoulder and leveled at them. Randy decided to take that one first.

'Stand and deliver!' the holdup man shouted theatrically, and Barry whipped his team forward as Randy cut loose with the left barrel of his double-twelve shotgun. The would-be robber was blown backward to sit hard on his rump and then roll onto his side as the stagecoach's wheels rolled over him.

Behind them the other man had mounted a hidden horse and now was driving down on them. Randy knelt on the seat of the swaying, lurching coach and loosed another load of double-ought buckshot from his express gun. He scored a hit — he could tell by the way the robber twisted in his saddle — but it was not a killing shot, and Randy ducked as he fumbled for two more shotgun shells. Cracking the weapon open he ejected the two still-smoking brass shells and reloaded.

The rider behind them was firing with his handgun. The wild fury of his attack made Randy think the robber was frustrated and angry. His reckless-ness put an end to the attack. Holding as steady as he could as the coach rumbled on, Randy cut loose with both barrels and the man was blown from the saddle to hit the ground rolling and tumbling. His strangely-familiar horse side-stepped away, slowed and halted, its head hanging.

'Get him?' Barry whose attention had been on his driving, asked.

'About as good as a man could be got,' Randy said, reloading again. Four ounces of double-ought buckshot assured that the man would not be rising from his wounds.

Barry Hampton nodded and began drawing back on the reins, slowing his team. Randy looked at him questioningly as the horses halted on the sunny crest of the hill.

'We should search them,' Barry said. 'The stage line and the local law always are interested in who might be pulling these hold-ups.'

'All right,' Randy agreed, although he was not eager to paw over the two dead men. Barry looped the reins around the brake handle and slid to the ground. Randy following him, noticing a single sentinel pine growing upslope from where they had halted, a golden eagle circling against the clear sky.

Together they walked to where the man who had taken a double load of shotgun pellets lay twisted against the earth. Randy still carried his weapon at the ready, listening, searching the barren landscape for others of the gang, if others there were. Barry crouched beside the dead man, patted his pockets and then toed him, rolling him onto his back. Randy caught his breath as the dead face appeared, dead eyes staring up at the morning sunlight. Barry Hampton looked at him curiously.

'Do you recognize him?' he asked from his crouching position.

'Yes. Yes, I do. His name is Tioga. We worked horses together once.'

What was Tioga doing up here trying to rob a stage? Had Van Connely and the rest of the gang decided to cut him out of the profit to be made from selling the herd?

They walked back to the first man

who lay on his side in the mud. Randy already knew before he too was rolled onto his back: it was Shell Bodine, another of the horse thieves.

'Nothing in his pockets either. Not a nickel. You knew him as well?' Barry asked, tugging his hat down to shade his eyes.

'Yes I did,' Randy said. 'At least well enough to identify. You see we had some trouble down the road,' and he went on to give Barry a brief sketch of the trail drive and murder of Skyler Lynch.

'So you think it was a falling-out among thieves; these two never got their cut from Van Connely?'

'That's all I can figure. If they had gotten their money, they'd be celebrating somewhere, not out trying to rob the Colton stage.'

'I guess you're right, but I guess we'll never know for sure.'

'No.'

'Your friend's still with us,' Barry Hampton said, and Randy turned to see the black stallion standing a short distance off. 'Do you want to try to throw a noose over its neck and tie it on behind?' the stage driver asked.

'Only if you need some entertainment for the rest of the day.'

Barry laughed. 'No, I guess I don't. Let's get going then. I still have a schedule.'

* * *

It was on a Saturday with a colorless sky spread overhead that Kate Lynch lifted her head to see the lone rider approaching the ranch. The two horses in the pole corral lifted their heads to study the newcomer as well. It was still cool, and smoke rose from the chimney of the stone house to drift and dissipate over the live-oak trees in the yard. Kate, who had been crouched tending to her poor effort at a flower garden, stood, dusting her hands together. She wore a tan-colored divided riding skirt and a peacock-blue blouse.

81

She waited, squinting into the distance, hoping to see other men following this single rider, but he was alone. Hesitantly she started across the yard. She thought she had seen this man before, but could not immediately name him. Young, but not so very young, he had dark hair that curled out where it escaped his hat, slender build with broad shoulders, even features and striking blue eyes. He rode a black horse with a white blaze and one white stocking. A beautiful animal, it moved at an easy long-legged gait. Its dark coat was like liquid obsidian; its muscles rippled beneath the skin. The lone rider approached her, halting the horse, tilting his hat back.

'Kate Lynch? My name is Randy Staggs. We've met once before — your father brought me over for dinner.'

'Oh, yes. I remember now. You were going along on the ride north with him.'

'That's right.'

'But where is . . . ?' she lifted her eyes to the distance.

'That's something we have to talk about,' Randy said in a tone of voice indicating he did not wish to talk about it. Kate shuddered slightly. A cold feeling was creeping over her.

'All right. Come inside and sit down. I have some coffee boiling.'

'Thank you. Mind if I put my horse up first.'

'Put him in the corral — he's a fine-looking fellow, isn't he?' she said admiringly.

'Yes. He's not really mine. As a matter of fact, he probably belongs to you,' Randy told her. 'That's another thing we need to talk about.'

'Unsaddle him, then,' Kate said, her voice trembling a little. 'I'll see to the coffee.'

Randy swung down and led the black to the corral. Uncinching his saddle, he reflected on Kate Lynch. She was smaller than he remembered. She had a pretty face, a full underlip and slight overbite which he found appealing. Dark hair just barely reaching her shoulders, a nicely modulated voice. And those nearly black eyes seeming fearful, proud, and confident at once. Randy wondered if she were part Indian. He could never remember Skyler Lynch saying a word about the girl's mother.

Slipping the bit from the horse's mouth, he released it into the corral. The black horse backed away from him uncertainly as if it suspected it was about to be abandoned again.

Randy had never thought he would end up riding the horse, contrary devil that it was. But afoot again in Colton, he had decided one morning to do something with the animal. It was that or give it up for dog meat. They had had a rugged time of it, from the first rope Randy had looped over the black's neck.

It had fought tooth and nail. When, on the second morning, Randy had actually managed to climb into the saddle, the black had crow-hopped, side twisted, reared up and jolted him down with both of its forelegs locked. Spinning, it had thrown Randy three times that day. Stiff and sore, he had tried again on the third morning to mount the horse. He sat in the saddle waiting for the dynamite to go off, but surprisingly the black had given up on tricks. Somehow something had seeped through into the horse's mind, convincing him that this man wasn't going to hurt him; he just wanted a ride. It learned to mind the reins quickly and now it carried Randy proudly as if it had achieved great skills.

'You're all right,' Randy grumbled, patting its sleek neck. 'If I had ten of you, I'd give you all away rather than go through that again.'

Still the horse remained independent and some mornings it had to be cajoled, wheedled, bribed into accepting the bit. A few men had tried to convince Randy that it was only because he was still partly wild, and that in time the black would become docile. Randy doubted it, but the horse let him ride, and moved with smooth energy. He was actually becoming fond of the old reprobate.

Randy swung the gate to the corral shut and hooked over the wire loop which held it in place while the black studied him with misgivings. Randy sighed, looked up at the sky and toward the distant bulk of the high mountains, their flanks glistening silver where the sunlight caught the run-off from the recent rain.

He crossed the yard to the ranch house as a cloud-shadow drifted past, went up onto the porch, rapped on the doorframe and went in. There was nothing he wanted to do less than tell Kate her father was dead, but she had to already know that. Why else would he have ridden in alone? He found her in the kitchen where the fragrance of dark coffee was heavy, and she turned with a smile. Gesturing toward the old plank table, she said, 'Be right with you.'

There was no cheer in her smile — it was a lost, sort of hopeful expression. While Kate shuffled cups and pot around, Randy dug into his pockets and pulled out the $180 in gold pieces he had left. Sunlight through the curtained kitchen window gleamed on the stacked coins, but it was a cold gleam as if the money no longer held the bright promise it once had.

'Here you go,' Kate said, offering Randy a cup of coffee. Then she caught sight of the coins and paused. 'What's this?' she asked.

'I told Skyler that I would bring it to you. The horses, as you might have figured, are gone. He had saved this aside just in case . . . so that you would have money for a fare East.'

Kate held up a hand, making a small pushing gesture. Then she sat in a chair facing Randy Staggs and said: 'Tell me about it, all of it.'

Randy nodded. Removing his hat he

leaned back a little in his chair, took a breath and told Kate everything that he had seen, all that had happened along the trail. When he was through, his coffee cup was empty. Empty as well were the dark eyes that Kate Lynch kept fixed on his face. He thought for a minute she was going to cry, but she seemed to be made of sterner stuff. She did sniff as she picked up a stack of coins and let them trickle through her fingers.

'The money will help out. There are some things I've been putting off buying until Father returned.'

'You're not going back East?'

'Why would I do that?' she asked, a little sharply. 'This is our . . . my land, and though it may not look like much, it is still my home.'

'Have you anyone to help you?'

'I haven't been able to afford anyone — besides, as you may have learned, honest men are hard to find around the Pocono. Else my father wouldn't have ended up hiring those . . . men that he was forced to.'

'He didn't have any choice, Kate. He had a chance to make some decent money — for himself, and for you. He knew it was a risk, but he took it.'

'For me. For the ranch,' Kate said, looking into her cup. 'Because he loved it.' Her eyes lifted again, 'Well I love it too, Randy, and no one, nothing is driving me off of it.'

'I can stay around for a couple of days and give you some help with the heavy work — if you want. I'm in no hurry to get anywhere.' He grinned, 'Especially since I have no idea where I'm going.'

'You're going to go after those men, aren't you?' she asked with a little touch of anxiety in her voice.

'Yes,' he said after a thoughtful pause. 'I suppose that's what I'm going to be doing.'

'How can you hope to find them, Randy? Do you mean to comb the entire territory, searching them out?'

'That, if I have to. And if I still can't find them I'll rake hell for them.'

5

The town was called Cameron Corners according to a crudely-painted sign at the town limits. Van Connely, riding a gray horse, led his group of four men up the rutted main street where pools of water still stood from the storm and set his eyes on a false-fronted building which advertised itself as a hotel. Sun-faded yellow paint peeled off the walls. It didn't look like much, but they were all tired of spending nights in the open.

'Well?' Connely called as they approached the hotel.

'We're not going to find anything better,' Archie Slater answered, and so the four men drew their horses up in front of the hitching rail and swung down.

'I say we get a few beers first,' Shawnee Burns said, standing, his hat tugged down against the sun, his horse's reins trailing from his thick hand. 'The hotel's not going anywhere.'

'Neither is the beer,' Van Connely reminded him, but he knew Shawnee's ways, his priorities. 'You might as well go where you like — we'll get a room for you two.' He hadn't bothered to ask Trapper McGee if he was going along, the long-haired man was utterly and inexplicably devoted to Shawnee.

As the two men swung into leather again and started on, seeking out a saloon, Slater dusted off his pants with his hands, tied his pony and started up onto the hotel porch. He said nothing as Van walked into the hotel with him. Van had still not figured out Slater, but he was good with a gun, and that was enough — his secrets could remain his own.

Van took three rooms side by side, mentally counting his reserves as he paid for them. They were getting low on cash money. Something had to be done about that. As he waited for the hotel boy to return with his gray suit, sent out to be brushed and pressed, Van stood at the window, looking out across the raw country.

He knew it had been a mistake to sell the horses as cheaply as they had, but the man from New Mexico Territory had cash and was willing to buy. Besides none of the remaining four members of the gang was willing to herd those horses along the trail, seeking a richer buyer. The defection of Bodine and Tioga had made everyone's work doubly hard. Bodine had gotten to where he could not take any more of Shawnee's riding and had announced that he was through. Tioga declared that he had taken enough bullying, too. The two had come to Van and laughably asked for money, offering their share of the sale in exchange.

Van said he hoped to see them again in better times, and the two disgruntled men had ridden off to seek their fortune somewhere else. It made the split larger for those who remained, but also left them with a hell of a job. Van had decided it was best to dump the HF-connected horses with the first buyer he came across without bothering to haggle over the price. Now, as he considered how little he had remaining, he found himself thinking twice. The man from New Mexico must be thinking of himself as one sharp horse trader — or maybe he was wise to the fact that the horses were stolen all along. He certainly didn't bother to ask for a bill of sale.

There was a light tap at the door and Van opened it to find a small dark-eyed kid standing there with his suit. He gave the boy a dime and closed the door, feeling better about the world as he took the suit and laid it on the rickety hotel bed. The town suit always did that for him. Duded up, shaved, he became again the man he thought himself to be.

And who knew? One good night at the card table or at roulette and his pockets might well again be lined with other men's money. Van unpeeled his trail shirt and began to whistle softly as he dug his razor out of his saddle-bags.

'You going out with me?' Van asked Slater who was sitting in his room, cleaning his revolver.

'I don't play cards,' Slater said, barely lifting his eyes.

'You could catch up with Shawnee and Trapper,' Van suggested.

'I seen Shawnee drunk before — it wouldn't be much entertainment.'

Van nodded and left the hawk-nosed man alone with his own thoughts. To hell with that, Van was thinking as he crossed the lobby of the hotel, heels clicking on the bare wood. He had the idea that this was going to be his lucky night, and he wanted no dark thoughts crowding into his bright state of mind.

There were two saloons facing each other across the rutted street. The one opposite was going great guns. Men whooped and shouted and cursed. The establishment on Van's side of the street was more sedate. It had harlequin-patterned half-glass and a newly varnished door with a brass handle. The set-up reminded Van of Morrisburg where the main street seemed to be the boundary between common riffraff and whatever gentlemanly clientele might be found on this side. Perhaps that was a common arrangement in this part of the country — give the lower class their own bar where they could get as drunk as they wished, brawl and break the furnishings while self-styled gentlemen willing and able to pay more for their entertainment expected and got a little more decorum.

Van Connely knew that he felt more at home dressed in his best than shouldering his way through a bunch of rough, trail-dusty men to get a glass of raw whiskey. He felt that way now, as he entered the saloon, and felt more comfortable immediately as he heard the soft whirring of a spinning roulette wheel, the familiar rattling of dice and noticed the well-dressed men seated around octagonal, baize-faced poker tables.

* * *

At the saloon called the Desert Regal, Shawnee Burns was sharing a table with Trapper McGee and scowling deeply at someone across the room. It was a crowded noisy place, alive with a lot of cursing and raised voices trying to be heard. Somehow amid the throng, Shawnee had managed to pick out one man standing at the bar, drinking from a mug of beer. He seemed to be about thirty years of age, had shaggily cut dark hair and dull eyes. He wore his brown Stetson tipped well back and had one boot resting on the brass rail beneath the bar.

'There — he did it again,' Shawnee said, still watching the man at the bar.

Trapper McGee looked at his long-time trail mate. This was all too familiar to Trapper. By the time Shawnee got past his third drink he began seeing potential enemies everywhere.

'What's he doing?' Trapper asked, sweeping his long hair back.

'Just looking at me, that's what.'

'Everyone's got to be looking somewhere,' was Trapper's bland response. He knew that would do nothing to calm Shawnee. Trapper stroked his long mustache and fingered the smudge of a beard he wore beneath his lip.

'He don't have to be looking at me!' Shawnee snarled. 'Let him look somewhere else. He probably thinks he's a tough man.'

'Probably thinks he might know you — that you look like someone he's seen before,' Trapper tried, knowing that it would do no good. When Shawnee got the idea in his mind that someone was his enemy, it stuck there good and proper.

'You know — I might have seen him before, Trapper. Down in Alamogordo. Remember that ugly stud who tried to face me down back there?'

Trapper shifted in his chair and

looked at the man at the bar who was now studying his own reflection in the saloon mirror. 'No, that's not him,' he told Shawnee definitely.

'Are you sure?'

'I'm sure.'

'Well, whoever he is he's staring at me,' Shawnee rumbled.

Trapper shrugged and remained silent. He had never had any luck trying to soothe Shawnee when he got like this. 'Want another drink? I'll go get 'em.'

Shawnee only nodded. Trapper rose and wove his way through the mob scene, passing the man at the bar. He was still staring at the mirror. Trapper wondered, not for the first time, why they put mirrors in saloons. Who wants to watch himself get slowly drunk? Reaching a bartender, Trapper ordered two more drinks. It made more sense to just buy a bottle rather than forcing his way through the crowd for refills, but it was never a great idea to spot a bottle down in front of Shawnee Burns. That only accelerated things, and Shawnee's fuse was already lit.

When Trapper returned to the table, Shawnee was still glowering, rubbing his stubbled chin with a thumb and forefinger. 'Did you tell him to stop it?' he asked as Trapper slid onto his chair.

'I didn't talk to him.'

He urged Shawnee to accept his fresh whiskey; sometimes liquor could reverse the process, leaving Shawnee in an expansive, overtly friendly mood. Then he would crowd up on strangers, throw his arm over their shoulders and tell them what fine fellows they were. It didn't look like that was going to happen tonight.

'He's walking out on me!' Shawnee said angrily, and Trapper lifted his eyes to see the stranger shouldering his way through the crowd toward the front door. 'He didn't even have the nerve to face me.'

'Let him go,' Trapper advised. 'It isn't worth it.'

'It wasn't you he was disrespecting,' Shawnee said, finishing off his whiskey, slapping the glass down on the table. He hesitated only a second and then rose heavily to his feet and started toward the door. Trapper silently sighed and followed Shawnee.

Outside the saloon the sun was bright and white, stunning their vision. Trapper could see a lone cowhand tying his horse to a rail opposite, a town couple in a surrey whirring past, on the opposite boardwalk a woman walking, carrying a bundle. And the man from the bar.

Shawnee had seen him first. He stepped down from the porch and yelled for the man to stop. Surprised, the man turned their way, and whatever the stranger's intent, Shawnee took it as cause to draw and fire. With his eyes still not adjusted to the brilliant daylight, Shawnee's first hastily fired shot went wild. Trapper saw the woman with the bundle throw up her hands, losing the bundle she had been carrying. Simultaneously, Shawnee fired again as the stranger, realizing that he was the target, pawed futilely at his own holstered weapon.

Shawnee's second shot caught its mark, and the man buckled to his knees in the street, dropping his unfired gun. Shawnee strode that way, firing as he went. Men boiled out of the saloon to see what was happening. Trapper backed away from the crowd, drawing his Colt to keep them back.

Across the street the woman was crying, and there was a thin, disturbing wailing in the air. Trapper was halfway across the street before he recognized the woman's dropped bundle for what it was — a baby wrapped in a blanket, lying on the rough plankwalk.

She looked up with anguished eyes as Trapper passed, her hands clasped prayerfully. There was a spot of red on the arm of her white blouse. The baby did not seem hurt, but it was raising a bawling fuss. Shawnee had ducked up an alley and Trapper hot-footed it toward the hotel as townspeople began to mill, looking up and down the street, a few crouched over the wounded woman, some shouting, pointing to the alleyway.

No one was pursuing Trapper and so he headed towards Van Connely's hotel room. Van was going to be mad as hell when he learned what Shawnee had done. Deciding to wait for Van's return, he went to the door of Connely's room. It stood open an inch. Trapper eased through it to find Van Connety already there, speaking with the deep-eyed Archie Slater. Van glanced at Trapper and then went on with what was apparently a long diatribe.

'That roulette wheel was fixed, I tell you. I been around enough wheels in my time to know when something's not right. I dropped a chip and looked for the pedal, but didn't see one right off. A few minutes later I went broke playing black six times in a row, and when I complained they muscled me out the door and onto the street. Well?' he snapped at Trapper. 'What do you want?'

'Me and Shawnee have to clear town, Van. Shawnee — you know how he is — he got into a shooting mess up the street.'

Van fell silent, rumpling his hair. He stood, took off his gray coat and unbuttoned his vest. Finally he answered, his eyes holding that unholy gleam that meant someone was in for trouble. 'All right,' he said quietly. 'Are you ready to ride, Slater?'

'I'm always ready, Van. I don't take no place as a permanent residence.'

'All right — you two head for the stable. Bring our horses to the back of the hotel. I'll wait for Shawnee. He's bound to show up soon. We'll meet you there.'

When the two had left, Van Connely finished undressing, cursing Shawnee Burns, the town of Cameron Corners, and the universe at large indiscriminately.

When Shawnee did appear, breathless and wild-eyed several minutes later, Van had already repacked his bag and drawn on his riding boots. The big man stood in the doorway, hat in his hands like a miscreant schoolboy and panted:

'Van, I had a little trouble . . . '

'Trapper already told me. Grab your bedroll. They'll have the horses out back waiting for us.'

Shawnee breathed a sigh of relief and walked hurriedly to his own room. He had been expecting a dressing-down from Van Connely, perhaps worse. Van seemed little troubled by events. At least he was nowhere as angry as he usually got when Shawnee stumbled into trouble. Shawnee grabbed his bedroll and slunk back down the hallway, looking for, listening for any signs of a pursuing band of men.

People had been lynched for less than the accidental shooting of a woman.

Van met him in the corridor, wearing his red and yellow-checked flannel shirt and dusty trail Stetson. Oddly, he carried a kerosene lamp that had been in the hotel room. 'This way,' Van told him as the two men heard the front door to the saloon bang open and a crowd of men surge through, shouting angry questions.

'That door,' Van said, gesturing. 'It leads to the back alley steps.'

Shawnee nodded appreciating Connely's thoroughness once again. While Shawnee had been thinking about alcohol, Van Connely had been planning ahead, scouting out the building in case they needed an escape route. They plunged through the door and down the outside steps as the sound of angry men grew louder inside. Below, Trapper and Archie Slater sat their horses, holding the reins to two other mounts. All of these horses wore the HF-connected brand. Their own horses had been pretty well tired out after the long drive from the north country, and they had selected four of the best from the herd before selling the rest to the New Mexican.

'Which way?' Slater asked and Van replied:

'Up the alley. That way.'

'That's taking us back to the center of town,' Trapper objected.

'And so?' Van asked challengingly, his eyes again darkening. His jaw was set, his mind made up. No one argued with Van Connely; they simply turned their horses' heads and rode up the alley. Half a block from the gambling house, Van removed the chimney from the lamp he had been carrying and unscrewed the cap from the filler tube. Tossing both aside, he struck a match and lit the wick. Trapper and Shawnee Burns looked at each other.

'Kick in the back door, Slater,' Van commanded, and Archie Slater swung down, approaching the rear door of the gambling house on foot. Having done that he returned to his horse as Van Connely kneed his gray horse forward and hurled the lantern inside. The kerosene spilled from the reservoir, spread across the wooden floor and caught fire. In seconds the red-gold flames curling up from the floor touched the dry wood of the walls and crept toward the ceiling. Someone appeared from an inner door, shouted and backed quickly away.

Cases of liquor stored in the room caught fire and went off like so many bombs. The windows were blown out and the flames mounted higher. By the time Van Connely and his men rode out of town, huge flakes of black ash carried high on funnels of heat sifted through the air. Looking back they could see the building, completely engulfed in flames, crackling and sagging to its death.

Van Connely halted, lit a cigar and muttered, 'That's all I had to say to them.'

They started on, toward the rough country beyond.

* * *

That night as they camped on a low knoll where bunch grass grew among the rocks Archie Slater eased over to where Van Connely sat smoking the second half of his cigar. Crouching down beside Van, he said, 'This can't go on for long, Connely.'

'What do you mean?'

'I mean we're spending more than we are making. What we got for the horses was hardly worth the days we spent on the trail pushing them south. The last week — well, after what we spent to pay for hotel rooms, meals, liquor and women — we're down to the point where we're going to have to make some money or break the gang up.'

'What have you got in mind?' Van asked, because obviously the brooding gunman had been giving it some thought.

'A bank,' Archie Slater said, lifting his eyes to see if the others could hear him. Shawnee and Trapper appeared to be sound asleep. The horses nosed at the bunch grass without much enthusiasm. 'I'm thinking we take our time and find a little town, check out the bank and the local law and grab what we can.'

'It's an idea,' Van said. 'Have you hit a bank before, Slater?'

'Two or three. There's not much in these small town banks, but they usually don't have much in the way of security either.'

'You're right. I once thought of hitting a saloon for their till, but there were twenty, thirty men in there — I don't think anyone tries saloons much. A little cracker-box bank, though — that might be just the ticket.'

'It'll see us along the way while we keep our eyes open for a bigger score.'

'I think you're right. How many towns are there out here?'

'Who knows? There's dozens of little settlements where the folks are so poor that they steal from their dogs. As far as where there's a place large enough to have a bank, I couldn't say. We'll just have to ride until we find the right set-up,' Slater said, rising.

'Try to keep Shawnee from drinking,' Van Connely said.

Slater laughed. 'And when I'm through with that, I'll try to keep the sun from rising.'

'Sooner or later he's going to mean trouble — not just for himself, but for all of us,' Van said gloomily. 'Try to slow him down a little. It's that or we're going to have to leave him behind.'

'That would mean losing Trapper, too,' Slater said, shaking his head. 'We don't have enough men as it is.'

'There's always men to be found,' Van Connely said, yawning. 'If we need them, we'll find them. For now just keep an eye on Shawnee, if you can.'

'If I can,' Slater agreed, although he knew that it was virtually impossible. If it came down to it, he decided, he would eliminate Shawnee Burns himself — the man was a walking liability. Slater had walked a risky path all of his life. There was no point in carrying his own risk with him. He had some loyalty to Van Connely, none to the others. He had made out just fine on his own before he had run into them; he would do so again, if it came to that.

* * *

110

Hazlit, the town was called. They came upon it the morning after next while the sky behind them marked red scars against the low gray clouds. There were fifty or so scattered buildings. A flat, lazy slate-gray creek meandered past west of town.

'Looks fairly prosperous,' Slater said to Van Connely.

'It's worth looking over,' Van answered with a satisfied nod of his head.

'I'm getting hungry,' Shawnee Burns said, halting his roan horse beside them. 'How about it, Van?' Van nodded even knowing that what Shawnee wanted came not on a breakfast plate but in a bottle. He had already decided to keep Burns in their hotel room or wherever they managed to find a place to sleep. Let him stay inside with Trapper; if he was cooped up they wouldn't have to worry about him, and Van and Slater could take care of the business of scouting out the town.

Hazlit showed signs of promise.

A row of buildings staggered along

the main street, looking like a good wind could take them down, but the streets were fairly crowded with all varieties of people, some of them appearing prosperous. A third of the way along they came upon a squat wooden building with bars on the front windows and a sign announcing itself as the Bank of Hazlit. Van Connely and Slater glanced only briefly that way — there would be time to study it more closely later.

They did notice a large stack of yellow bricks in the alley beside the bank. These were intended, obviously, for improving the bank. It didn't bother Van Connely.

They would be finished with their business and gone long before the new brick building was constructed.

6

The morning was bright with color spraying through the patchy clouds when Randy Staggs stepped out of the house. Kate had been up for an hour, starting a fire to take the chill off the stone house. He stepped off the porch and walked to the pole corral. Two of the horses there came to meet him and thrust their muzzles over the rails hopefully. The black backed away to the farthest corner of the pen, eyeing him with suspicion.

'Not this morning,' Randy muttered, unhooking the wire loop holding the gate shut. 'I'm not in the mood for it.'

He was in fact planning to saddle the black horse and reluctantly ride west once more. The past few days had been lived as he would like to live them. Hot breakfast early in the morning, a solid day's work on various projects around the ranch and a large, if not fancy dinner with Kate Lynch sitting across the table from him. All things must pass, he reminded himself, and this was the morning he must leave that comfortable life.

'You are going to take this,' he threatened the black, approaching it with bridle and bit in hand. The black tossed its head and trotted along the side rails of the corral, forcing Randy to trek after it, cursing beneath his breath.

'You should have been riding him every day,' Randy heard Kate say behind him. She was just slipping through the gate, the other two horses nuzzling her. 'He's going wild again. Such a beautiful animal, he is,' she commented, moving toward the black which watched her approach with a sort of horse astonishment, its eyes rolling.

'So beautiful,' Kate said again as she reached the horse, which did not shy from her hand as she raised it to stroke its neck.

'Watch it,' Randy warned, 'he bites.'

'Why would he bite me?' she answered. To the horse: 'You wouldn't bite me, would you, big boy?' She stroked its muzzle and asked across her shoulder. 'Do you mind if I ride him for a bit — just around the corral?'

'If you can get this on him,' Randy said, holding up the bridle.

'Oh, I don't need that for a short ride,' she said and then, astonishing Randy, she gripped the black's mane and swung aboard almost effortlessly. As he stood watching in amazement, she heeled the black and started it forward at an easy trot. There was no bucking, no biting, no reluctance to mind this rider on the black's part.

They circled the pen twice and then Kate halted it in front of Randy Staggs, patting the horse's neck. 'He's some animal,' Kate said, slipping down from its glossy back.

Randy only muttered, 'He sure is.' He wasn't sure if he was angry with the black or jealous of Kate's horse skills. Maybe he had been right — the little dark-haired girl rode as if she were part Indian.

'Want me to slip him the bit?' she asked, smiling at Randy.

'I'll manage,' he replied dourly.

'Where are you going this morning?' Kate asked, for they hadn't discussed his departure. Randy had wanted to retain their false happiness for as long as possible, even though Kate knew that there would come a day when he would be leaving.

'Hunting, Kate. It's the day for it.'

'Oh, I see . . . ' and then she did see, and her smile faded to an unhappy frown. 'You mean — after *them*.'

'That's right,' he said, buckling the throat latch of the horse's bridle. He did not turn to face her. 'They killed your father, Kate. Someone has to make them pay for it, and there's no one else.'

'Oh, of course,' she answered hastily, shakily. 'I can see that . . . I've left the coffee boiling,' she said before starting toward the house. With her voice choking, she added, 'I'll make up a few sandwiches for you to eat along the trail.'

Randy stood watching her until she swept through the doorway, feeling that he was making a mistake, knowing he hadn't. Van Connely and his men must be stopped, must be brought to justice. And it was true — he was the only one to do the job. He walked back toward the house, leading the saddled, less recalcitrant black horse. Hitching it loosely, he went inside to see two cups of coffee on the table. Kate showed him only her back as she sliced bread with more motion than seemed necessary.

'Where will you start?' she asked, still keeping her eyes on her breadboard. 'The land is so vast.'

'I'll go back to a town called Blind Man's Spring first — I was told that a group of men with a herd of HF-connected horses had been through there. Someone must have seen them leave. It's hard to move secretively with forty horses to push.'

'Do you think they still have them?' Kate asked.

'I don't know,' Randy said, seating himself before his coffee cup. 'I would doubt it. They'll sell them off at first chance. They've no use for them, only for money.'

'Oh.' Kate seemed slightly disappointed, though she couldn't have sheltered much hope of ever seeing the other horses. Now she turned and sat down opposite Randy, crossing her forearms on the table. A smile returned briefly and then faded away again. 'It's going to be a long ride, isn't it?'

'Very long. I don't know if I have a chance of finding them, really.'

'Randy, maybe I should . . . do you think I should . . . ?'

'Go along with me?' he laughed, not with humor. 'Certainly not. Besides, the captain would want you to remain behind — since you refuse to go East and see to the ranch. You have a few dollars to buy yourself some necessities now. Don't think of such nonsense.'

'I know it's not reasonable,' Kate said, 'but I feel like I should do something. It's so frustrating just sitting here and — '

'You stood it while your father was gone. You're strong enough to do it now.'

'Yes, but I always thought Father would somehow make it back. You . . . you're not even thinking of returning, are you, Randy?'

He let her question fall into a silent abyss. No, he wasn't thinking of it. Even if he wanted to, there seemed little chance that he would ever be able to make it back alive.

'Take care of the ranch,' he said somewhat sternly, rising from the table. 'And . . . yourself.'

The black horse didn't fight as he mounted and turned its head away. Before he got far, Kate rushed out with a muslin bag containing three sandwiches and a few apples. These he tied onto his saddle-horn and started on his way again. As he cleared the yard,

Randy glanced back. He could still see Kate Lynch standing in the doorway. She waved, and he lifted his hand in her direction before heeling the black more roughly than he had intended, and riding it off across the broken ground toward the far away places.

*   *   *

Two days later Randy made his way to Blind Man's Springs. He paused on a knoll just south of the town and remembered how grateful he had been to come upon it after days of walking in the wilderness. Now it appeared in its real form: only a collection of gray weathered wood buildings, some seeming to tilt drunkenly on their foundations. The settlement's time was passing rapidly.

He found the stable again without difficulty. The same tall, narrow stablehand he had met on his last visit was there, sitting in front of the unpainted building on a wooden bench, warming himself in the sun.

'Help you?' the lanky man inquired around a yawn.

'Yes. I was through here about a week ago . . . '

'Were you?' the gangly stableman said. Rising he came nearer and then recognized not Randy, but the black horse. He smiled and then said apologetically. 'Now I recognize you — sorry, I remember horses a lot better than I recall people's faces. I see you managed to throw a saddle over the black. When he busted out of here I thought I'd never see him again. Don't tell me he started following you again after you got on the stage!'

'That's what he did. Finally I decided if I didn't own him, he thought he owned me, so I decided to keep him.'

'I see,' the man said dubiously, rubbing the black's flank. He was staring at something and now Randy saw what it was: the HF-connected brand. 'Those are the boys we had trouble with — they were riding horses

121

with that brand.'

'You told me that before. Now I'd like to ask you some questions about them,' Randy said, swinging down from the horse's back.

'Oh, you would? Do you want me to tend your horse?' he asked taking the bridle.

'Please. He could use a good rub. It was a long trail with little forage or water. You'd think that as hard as it rained there would be standing water somewhere.'

'Land soaks it up like a sponge,' the stable-hand said, leading the black inside the stable. 'You know, mister, you told me when you were here last that the horse wasn't yours. It had just sort of followed you. I believed you. Then after you took the stagecoach out of here, I started to wonder if you weren't just ridding yourself of him so as not to be tied in with the rest of that HF-connected bunch.'

'I can see that might occur to you, but I'm not one of them,' Randy answered, sitting on a nail keg as the horse was put in a stall, its saddle removed. 'Like I said, I would like to ask you a few questions about them.'

'Hunting them are you?'

'I guess you'd have to say that. Those boys wronged me.'

'They wronged everybody they came across in Blind Man's Springs. One of them — a big, chunky man — half tore up our little saloon.'

That would be Shawnee Burns, Randy thought. Aloud he said: 'I was wishing to know which way they went from here.'

'I can tell you what I heard,' the stable-hand answered, taking the black horse a bucket of water. 'Cole Freeman is a good friend of mine. He says he saw them camped out a little south of here. They were meeting up with some man Cole knows from New Mexico — a horse trader. He thinks they sold the herd to him then rode south and west, in the direction of Cameron Corners. Know where that is?'

'No,' Randy answered.

'About twenty miles from here, it's a pretty well-traveled road. Someone along the way will be able to point you right.'

'Thank you. Feed the black, will you? I've got to find some chow for myself. Is Mae Lincoln still running that restaurant?'

'Mae?' the stable-hand gave a muffled snort. 'Of course she is! Where else would she go? Where can anyone in this town go? We're all stuck here until the day we die or the town blows away and dies itself. That's Blind Man's Springs for you,' he said, walking away, shaking his head.

Randy slipped off the keg and went out into the harsh sunlight of the day, walked the short distance to Mae Lincoln's restaurant and went inside. He still had fourteen dollars left from the twenty dollars he had chipped from Kate's fortune but hated to spend a cent of it; nevertheless it was eat or perish himself and so he took a seat at a small round table and waited for Mae.

She bustled up a few minutes later, pad in hand. It was obvious that she didn't recognize him either — Randy was beginning to feel like a ghost. As she took his order, he asked, 'Seen Barry Hampton around lately?'

'The stage driver?' Mae asked.

'Yes.'

'No, ain't seen him. Someone told me he got held up and shot on the Colton run. I heard they might have to take his leg off.'

'I hope not,' Randy said soberly. He had liked the stage driver. As he waited for Mae to return with his meal, he idly listened to conversation at the next table. He didn't get the gist of it, but one of them brought up the name of Cameron Corners. He waited for a pause in the conversation and then leaned back in his chair to ask:

'Pardon me, men — did I hear you mention Cameron Corners? I'm on my way there but seem to have lost my way.

Can you tell me where to find the road out?'

They did, if not affably, at least not in a hostile way. These two, whoever they were, seemed to be carrying some trouble of their own. After they had given Randy instructions, the older one, the one with the handlebar mustache told him:

'You won't find the town at its best right now. Everyone's a little upset. Some lunatic tried to burn the whole town down.'

Randy only frowned with his eyebrows and left the two to their private conversation. It was of no concern to him — or was it? He knew one man who had taken out his anger with a town using violent methods: Van Connely.

He wondered . . . he had been told that the gang was riding toward Cameron Corners not a week ago. Was it possible that they were the ones responsible for the fire? He wanted to ask the two men some more questions, but he had bothered them enough, and anyway they were just rising from their table as Mae returned with a platter of potatoes and eggs for Randy. There would be time enough to ask questions once he reached Cameron Corners.

Wasting still more of his money, Randy again took a room in the tumbledown hotel. He had to have some sleep, at least a few hours, and it wouldn't hurt to have the black horse well rested for the next leg of the trip. He thought of many things as he lay on the sagging bed, watching the ceiling for a long while. After a time he finally managed to close his eyes and drift off into a weary sleep. He found himself thinking about only one thing before his dream, during his dream and after his dream.

Kate Lynch.

He could picture almost perfectly her bright smile, full lower lip, her slight overbite and dark eyes which always seemed merry or astonished, depending on her mood. Would the image of her fade before he had completed his mission, or would it just fade to nothingness when he failed at his task?

* * *

Cameron Corners, when Randy Staggs reached it late the next afternoon he found was a little larger than Blind Man's Springs, but not much prettier. There was an odd torpor about the people he passed and a strange smell in the air which it took him a while to recognize — the scent of dead fire.

Farther along the street he saw the fire-gutted saloon, its roof sagged in on black ashes. The buildings on either side of the saloon had been touched by flames as well. One of them — a saddlery, had two men at work on it, crow-barring scorched siding planks from the wall. There were few people walking the streets. It was almost as if they were hiding after the attack of an invading army.

Randy could see Van Connely doing

such a thing, heedless of any people who might be killed or injured in the aftermath, but he could not figure why the outlaw would have done it. No matter — it took very little to set Connely off. He was almost as bad as Shawnee Burns when you came down to it, though Van would have argued the point vehemently. Yet Burns, violent as he was usually picked out one unsuspecting citizen for his murderous ways. Van Connely had nothing against killing an entire town if he thought he had been affronted.

It took Randy a while to find the stable — this one was set well away from the town, the civic planners having recognized the undesirability of dung-smell and horse flies at its center. A creek, narrow and shallow wound past Cameron Corners and nearly at its edge was a horse pen. There was also a small, low barn before which three saddled horses stood dozing in the sun. Randy turned his black that way. As he approached, three men exited the barn and moved toward the horses. One of them was wearing a badge which gleamed in the sunlight as he turned to look at the incoming rider.

Frowning, the lawman said something in a low voice to his companions and unbuttoned his coat to reveal a low-riding Colt. Randy saw all of this, but paid it no mind. It could have nothing to do with him. Probably the men were just wary of strangers which was common in these far-flung settlements.

'Good morning,' Randy called cheerfully as he drew up the black and glanced around.

'Stable-hand around?'

'Yeah,' one of them — a man with an abnormally large head — said. 'Swing down, I'll find him for you.'

The other stranger, a buck-toothed kid with a knobby nose, smiled back at Randy, but it was an idiot's smile, as if the kid were not quite right. The lawman, a broad-shouldered man of middle years sporting a wild gray mustache, said nothing as Randy stepped out of the saddle. The man who had said he was going to find the stable-hand had not taken a step, Randy noticed. Randy frowned and felt tension creep up his spine. There was trouble in this town, that was obvious, but he had nothing to do with any of it, and so he loosened the cinches on his horse while the others moved nearer.

'Nice horse,' the sheriff said, finally speaking. His voice was gravelly, low pitched.

'He gets me where I'm going,' Randy said.

'He'll get you there, all right,' the town marshal said. 'Because you won't be going far. Only over to the jail.'

'Me . . . ' Randy dropped the stirrup he had been lowering. 'What for? You must have me mistaken for someone else. I've never been in Cameron Corners before in my life. I can't imagine what this is about.'

'No?' the marshal said, now standing beside him. His stubby finger reached out and tapped the black horse's flank as he smiled menacingly at Randy. 'Try imagining a little harder.'

Randy shook his head in puzzlement and then frowned as he saw where the marshal's finger had settled. Their eyes met and the marshal smiled again, less convincingly. His finger was firmly placed, indicating the brand on the black's flank:

HF.

7

Randy moved, but not as quickly as the man with the bald, pumpkin-sized head who raised his rifle and brought the stock down on Randy's skull or the marshal who was there quick enough to keep Randy from falling to the ground as the multicolored stars began dancing behind his eyes. Randy's last vision before tumbling into a well of blackness was of the goofy-looking kid dancing a wild joyful jig as he was beaten down.

The next time Randy saw daylight it was through a barred window. His head throbbed. Peering at the sun caused saber-like pain to drive through his skull. When he was able to sit up he found himself on a wooden cot hanging from two chains attached to the wall of a brick building. He sat bowed over, holding his head for a long while, scarcely aware of the marshal with the huge mustache who had drawn a wooden chair over to seat himself beside the cell.

'Good, you are alive,' the marshal said in his gravelly voice. 'I was afraid that Hardy had hit you too hard.' Then: 'You'll live long enough to hang.'

'Hang?' Randy said numbly. He was more offended than angry as he lifted his head and looked through the cell bars at the lawman. 'I didn't do anything.'

'Never had a prisoner plead guilty yet,' the marshal said. 'Guess what — almost all of them are proved to be.' He leaned nearer to the bars of the cell. Outside, Randy could hear the squawks of quarreling crows in a broken oak tree.

'Son,' the marshal continued. 'Cameron Corners might seem like a jerkwater town — all right, it is — but it's my town, and I do my best to protect it. Bunch of men trying to burn the place down doesn't set right with me. As for any jury you might come up before, they won't have a qualm in the world about hanging you for it.'

'I wasn't with them!' Randy objected loudly. He lowered his voice. Shouting caused the pain to flare up again. 'I'm on their trail, trying to catch up with them.'

'I don't see how you planned to do that. And I know you won't do it from where you are now.'

'I don't either,' Randy said truthfully. 'It's just something I have to do. I'll find them if I need to track them to the gates of hell.'

The marshal nodded thoughtfully, then smiled unevenly. 'Right now,' he replied, 'it seems you'll be in hell long before they are, waiting to greet them.' He rose from his chair. The wooden legs scraped on the plank floor. Randy cried out urgently:

'You're not giving me a fair chance, Marshal. If all you have on me in the way of evidence is the brand on my horse, I can explain that, if you'll just listen.'

The marshal nodded and then grudgingly took a seat again. 'All right. If you've got a story, I might as well listen to it.'

Taking a deep breath, Randy started at the beginning of the events which had brought him to Cameron Corners and talked through to the end, leaving no details out to try to make it sound more believable. Which it apparently did because the marshal nodded his head thoughtfully now and then, listening closely.

'You can name all these men?' the lawman asked when Randy was finished.

'Yes, I can give you all their names so that you'll be able to get posters out on them.'

'That would be helpful . . . assuming I can believe your story.' The marshal rose again. 'I don't know if I can,' he said. 'If everything you say is true — it would help your case if you just happened to have a bill of sale for those HF-connected ponies.'

Randy didn't smile. Smiling hurt. But he reached into his shirt and handed the marshal the much-folded bill of sale that he had taken from Skyler Lynch's coat pocket as he lay dying. The marshal studied it carefully, his eyes narrowing as he muttered, 'Well, well. Damn me, it seems we might have acted a little too hastily.' He handed the bill of sale back through the bars of the cell. 'I don't believe anyone could have made up such a complicated yarn as you've spun. If you were a part of that gang, you'd still be with them. If you're trying to run them to earth, of course you're just crazy but it seems to me,' he said with the first genuine smile Randy had seen, 'that you're doing this all for the girl. I suppose I can understand that kind of craziness, even at my age.'

Randy mumbled a reply and turned his eyes down. He heard metal clicking against metal, and when he looked up he saw the marshal turning the key in the lock of his cell. 'Let's you and me go and get something to eat. I need to talk to you a little more. I'll need the names and descriptions of those four and any other information you can give me about them. I appreciate that you want to hunt them down on your own, but you've got to admit that the law has a better chance of dealing with them like they deserve.

'I'll send Bobo over to fetch your horse.'

After a meal of ham, white grits and apple sauce shared with the marshal, Randy emerged into the purpling light of dusk to untie the black from the rail in front of the restaurant. It was late to continue his travels, but Randy wanted to get out of the marshal's sight and well away from Cameron Corners before darkness settled. Being alone on the desert would be a more comfortable place to be than the still-threatening town.

Swinging aboard the black, he rode out of the small town, past the burned buildings and away from the smoky smell of destruction.

To the horse he muttered, 'That was too close. How would you feel about getting your brand changed if we happen to run across some cinchring artist?' The black snorted as if with disgust and Randy patted its neck, moving on across the raw country, looking for a place to camp for the night.

★ ★ ★

'They did what?' Van Connely shouted angrily. Trapper McGee stood shame-faced before him, hat in hand, staring at the wall of the hotel room.

'They gave him ten days in jail,' Trapper said apologetically. He knew that it had been his job to keep an eye on Shawnee. It had gone well for a time. Locked up in their bedroom, they had brought whiskey to Burns so that he wouldn't go out looking for trouble.

'Me and Archie,' he said, nodding at Slater who sat coolly in a corner chair,

139

listening, watching with those deep-set eyes of his. 'Sometime after midnight Archie asked me could I handle things. Said he was going to catch some sleep. Well, Shawnee was snoring on his bed, so I said 'Sure, I can watch him', and so Archie went off to his own room.

'No sooner had the door closed than Shawnee sat up and swung his feet to the floor. 'Now we can find some action', he says.

'I couldn't stop him,' Trapper said miserably. 'No one can when he's had a few drinks and has his mind made up — you know that, Van.'

'Yeah,' Van Connely said darkly, 'I know that. Did you go along with him?'

'Well, I kind of had to — if I was going to keep an eye on him.'

'What did he do?'

Trapper looked at the toes of his boots and replied, 'Shot a man.' Trapper added hurriedly, 'He didn't hurt him much!'

'Just enough so that they threw him into jail?'

'Yeah,' Trapper said, trying a smile which had no effect on Van Connely's mood. The outlaw leader was silent for minutes, studying Trapper with disgust. The long-haired gunman shifted his feet uneasily.

'All right,' Van said abruptly. 'Go on back to your room and get some rest, Trapper.'

'What are we going to do about it?' Trapper McGee asked, his voice tentative.

'I haven't decided yet — scat.'

Trapper eased out of the room and closed the door quietly. Van rubbed a hand across his scalp and shook his head. 'I was about to lose my temper.'

'He had a point,' Slater said from his corner chair. 'Once Shawnee has his mind made up . . . What *are* we going to do about it, Van?'

'What do you recommend, Archie?' Van's voice was tinged with bitterness. 'We can't bust him out of that jail — not without wrecking everything we've been planning. Now that we've got the bank job set up, that would ruin us all.'

'Well, then — leave him to rot?'

'That would leave us short of men. Trapper would likely stick with Shawnee no matter what. That would leave only the two of us to stick up the bank. Think that's enough?'

'Two of us inside, no one to watch our backs and hold the horses? No, we planned out a four-man job.'

'And bringing in two new men at this late date is a bad idea. They'd have to be from this town, and we don't know any of these locals well enough to trust them.' Van went to the window and stared out at the nearly empty street. He had known this was going to happen, that Shawnee Burns was bound to throw a monkey-wrench into the works of their carefully thought-out scheme.

'It's my fault, I suppose,' Van said. 'I should have tied him up and locked him in a closet to dry out until it was time to stick up the bank.'

Archie Slater couldn't tell if Van was serious about such a wild plan or not. But it might have worked. It would have if Trapper wasn't so damned devoted to Shawnee — why exactly, no one could guess. But Shawnee seemed to be some sort of hero to the long-haired man. Something in their past neither had discussed, Slater guessed. Anyway, Shawnee always seemed to get his way whenever Trapper was involved. Shawnee could have talked his way out of something like that.

Slater stood and stretched. 'It's as much my fault,' he said. 'I should have stayed in the room, but Shawnee appeared to be asleep and I figured I'd need some rest if I was to be fresh in the morning. Now, it looks like it doesn't matter anymore. We can't hit that bank tomorrow — or ever. Think it over, Van, and let me know what you want to do. I'd be happy to find a new town.'

'And have Shawnee do the same thing all over again? No, Archie, we'll take that bank — we need the money — but I'll have to spend some time thinking it over now.'

'One of us will have to go over to the jail tomorrow and let Shawnee know we're standing with him. Otherwise he just might start talking too much.'

'I don't think he would ever . . . ' Van broke off his sentence and began thinking. Shawnee might do just that if he felt they were deserting him. That was too much of a risk to run.

But what if Shawnee was unable to talk? That would leave them with nothing to fear and still three men in the small gang. Enough to knock over that flimsy desert town bank. Van glanced up at Slater who had not left the room yet. 'I'll do some thinking, Archie. You get some sleep and we'll talk in the morning.'

Van Connely waited until Slater had been gone fifteen minutes, then walked to the head of his bed where he had slung his gunbelt around a bed post. Outside it was still hours before sunrise. The little town's streets were deserted. It was a good time of night to pay a visit to the town jail.

★ ★ ★

Shawnee Burns opened a bloodshot eye, hoping that the events of the night had been a dream. But the interior of the small jailhouse, illuminated only by the dim glow of the fading moon refuted that notion. His head was throbbing and there was no relief to be had. That damned little cowhand had the nerve to talk back to him, leaving him no choice but to draw and shoot. It hadn't been a good shot — only peeled a chunk of flesh off the other man's ribs. Then the entire saloon full of men had jumped him. Too many and too close for Trapper to help out with his own gun.

Dragged over here, the justice of the peace had sentenced Shawnee to ten days in jail, adding somberly that if the bullet had struck the stranger a few inches higher on his body, he would be sending for the hangman.

Shawnee found himself suddenly awake in the gloom, wondering what had caused him to come alert — if his fuzzy thoughts could be considered to be such. Whatever it was, the sound came again. He frowned. It was the sound of metal against metal, he was sure of that. He rose heavily from his cot, pain rampaging through his throbbing skull, and turned toward the moonlit window of his cell.

Approaching it carefully, he saw the barrel of a pistol again tap the black iron bars. There was someone out there and he risked peering out.

'Van!' he said with astonished pleasure.

'Keep your voice down, Shawnee,' Van Connely hissed.

'Sure. Are you boys gonna bust me out of here?'

'Not right now,' Van answered. 'But we have a plan. Come nearer and let me tell you.'

Shawnee hooked his meaty hands around the bars of the window and peered out at Van standing in the moonlit alley. 'What is it, Van?' he whispered. 'You're getting me out, right?'

'Shawnee, we decided you just aren't worth it.' The muzzle of the pistol exploded with flame, a .44 bullet punching through Shawnee Burns's forehead, sending him staggering across the cell to slump down against the door, quite dead.

Van ducked down, holstered his pistol and sprinted up the alley toward a side alley which led back to the hotel. His heart was pounding, his vision a little blurred from the surge of excitement, but he heard no one call out, saw no one rushing out to challenge him. Van slowed his pace to a walk, unholstered his revolver and flipped the empty shell casing away, reloading with a fresh cartridge. If anyone was suspected of the murder it would be the man Shawnee had shot, or perhaps one of his friends trying to get even. Not that anyone would be concerned enough about Burns to take the trouble to find out who had done it.

Van emerged from the alley onto the main street where all remained silent. Despite himself he found that he was smiling as he made his way back into the hotel lobby, nodded at the bleary-eyed clerk and climbed the stairs to his room.

* * *

Piece of cake. It was a piece of cake knocking over that cracker-box bank. They had scouted the place for days and knew that the portly little bank manager arrived at 9 a.m. every morning, his clerk half an hour later. The first customers never showed up before ten when the bank was officially open.

Trapper McGee held their horses in a side alley as Van and Archie Slater, timing it exactly, met each other from opposite ends of the plankwalk and greeted one another, talking about the weather, the grass and the price of cattle as the bank manager passed them with barely a glance and inserted the key into the front door of the bank.

Turning with guns drawn, Van and Archie followed on his heels before the round little man could close the door and lock it.

'What's this?' the banker asked. His hands were shaking.

'Don't waste time asking stupid questions,' Van Connely snapped. 'Just open up that vault.' Van wore no mask — they didn't figure to be around long enough for anyone to identify them, and his hard eyes and set mouth told the banker that it would be wise to obey. For added emphasis, Van cocked his revolver. 'I don't like making a lot of noise unless I have to,' he said, lifting the muzzle of his Colt until it was level with the bank manager's heart. 'Get on with it!'

The round little man fumbled with the combination of the safe for a few minutes, perhaps thinking help might arrive, but with the constant urging of Van's pistol, he eventually swung the door to the green safe wide. The banker was perspiring by then although the room was cool. He kept glancing at the brass-bound clock on the wall. 'Fifteen minutes before your teller gets here,' Van said. 'Besides, he won't be of any help to you. We've got men outside to keep him from walking in. Start filling these bags,' he added as Slater handed him two of the canvas pouches ordinarily used for making large transfers between banks.

The banker must have figured that there was no point in further delay, in risking the ire of the robbers, for he had the safe emptied, its contents transferred to the bags within five minutes. Van Connely watched him, sifting out property deeds, liens and loan agreements for which they had no use. Also he still was not sure there wasn't a hideaway gun secreted somewhere in the safe. It had been known to be done.

'Ten minutes,' Archie Slater said, glancing at the clock. 'We don't want to be here the one day the teller decides to show up early.'

'No,' Van agreed, placing the bags of cash and coin on the counter. 'Got anything to tie him up with?' he asked, nodding at the banker whose face was now glistening with perspiration.

'Why waste the time?' Slater said, and he slammed his pistol barrel against the banker's head just behind his ear, driving him to the floor, his eyes rolled back.

'Let's ride,' Connely said, snatching up one of the bags while Slater collected the other.

Outside, the morning sun was casting long shadows. Its glare was brilliant through the gaps between the buildings. A kid ran by rolling a hoop, another younger one ran after him screaming. Along the boardwalk they watched as the rail-thin man they knew to be the bank teller, strode toward the bank. Van and Slater scurried around the corner to take their horses' reins from Trapper McGee.

Exiting the alley onto the main street, Van saw the teller approaching the bank's door and he tipped his hat to the man who stood puzzled for a few minutes before entering. 'Walk 'em, boys,' Van said in a low taut voice as Trapper started to heel his long-legged roan horse into a run. 'Let's not draw more attention to ourselves.'

A long minute passed when presumably the bank teller tried to attend to his boss. Then the younger man emerged from the bank and yelled up and down the empty street for help. Before anyone could come forth to help him, the robbers were at the outskirts of town, passing through a large grove of cottonwood trees that grew along the creek. Van held the gang up for a minute before crossing the creek. Trapper McGee asked anxiously, 'What about Shawnee?'

'We'll come back for him,' Van assured him. 'We've got the money to put up bail now. In the meantime we should put a little distance between ourselves and the citizens of Hazlit.'

After they had started on Archie Slater asked Van, 'How much do you think we took?'

'Didn't have time to think about counting it,' Van Connely answered, 'but it sure is a hell of a lot more than we started the morning with. And it was easy, wasn't it?'

'Easy. Van, I think I could take a liking to this sort of work.' He nodded toward Trapper, riding a little away from them, 'What about him?'

'What do you mean?'

'When he finds out that we aren't going back for Shawnee.'

'I'll think of something to tell Trapper. A fistful of money should soften his regret, don't you think?'

'I'd think so,' Slater said with a thin smile. 'Cash always has a way of salving my conscience.'

'Mine too,' Van said. 'If it isn't enough for him, Trapper can go back and try to save Shawnee. Though I doubt he'll have much luck at that.' And they rode on, both smiling at Van's black humor.

8

When Randy Staggs dragged into Hazlit, he felt its dark mood as he walked the black along the street. It seemed the men he was following cast dark shadows everywhere they went. He did not know that the gang had passed through here, but he felt as if it were so. He stopped first at the office of the town marshal. Ordinarily he would have seen to his horse first, but there was a growing urgency within him to find Van Connely's gang. The long trail had not fostered frustration but determination. He had been only days behind them in Cameron Corners — if they had laid over in Hazlit for long, he could be right on their heels. The thought lifted his spirits but did nothing to quiet the notion that he was a fool on a fool's errand.

''Mornin',' Staggs said to the beefy

man who sat behind the scarred desk as he entered the office. The marshal glanced up but was not smiling. He wore a sagging expression as if the burden of his duties weighed heavily on him. In the corner sat another man, his face flushed so deeply that it nearly matched the color of his red hair. This one did nod to Randy.

'Is this important?' the marshal asked. 'Because if not, come back another time. I've got other things that need my attention.'

'What I need . . . ' Staggs began but the marshal continued his little speech without listening.

'A bank robbery and a man murdered in my own jail cell,' the lawman said. 'And election time coming up next month! So, young man,' he said, leaning back, his hands flat on his desk, his eyes now meeting Randy's, 'I can't offer much help right now whatever your problem is, and since you can't do anything for me, we'll have to have a conversation at another time.'

'Maybe I can,' Randy Staggs said, removing his hat for the first time.

'Can what?' the marshal asked.

'I may have some information that will help you — I'm not sure that it's connected, but it just may be.'

'Out with it then,' the lawman said almost angrily. He was obviously very disturbed by events.

'One thing first — can I take a look at the murdered man? I think that may clear matters up.'

The marshal sighed heavily, rising from his chair. 'He's still in the back. Sent for the mortician, but he hasn't come yet.'

Randy was led down a short corridor past the cell where evidence of blood still colored the plank floor, and into a small storage area. Shawnee Burns's face was not covered, and Randy only needed a quick glance to make his identification.

'That was a man you know?' the marshal asked. Randy nodded. 'Come and tell me about it, then. My name's

Traylor — sorry I was so abrupt, but this is a bad day for me and for Hazlit.'

Back in the office Randy pulled up another chair and faced Traylor across his desk. 'The dead man's name is Shawnee Burns,' he told the marshal. 'You'll likely get a circular on him in the next few days out of Cameron Corners. He was traveling with a gang of no-goods led by a man called Van Connely. There are a couple of others — I'll give you their names. If Burns was in Hazlit, the others likely were as well. You can ask at the hotel, any other place that might have seen them. I'll give you their descriptions.'

'You talk as if you know them well,' the red-faced man in the corner said.

'Too well,' Randy said. 'They've been raising hell in this part of the territory for weeks now. It's a good bet that they're the ones who knocked off the bank.'

'What about their friend back there?' the marshal asked, nodding in the direction of the room where Shawnee

Burns's body rested.

'I don't know,' Randy said honestly, 'except that Burns had a habit of stirring up trouble wherever he went. Looks as if Connely finally got tired of it.'

'I suppose that could be,' Traylor agreed. 'This Burns — if that's who he is — was shot at point blank range through the window. Somehow it doesn't seem that he'd have gone up there to meet someone he didn't know.'

'I have no proof, of course, but that's what I think happened, too. How many men were in on the bank job?'

'Three, as far as we know, which fits with what you are saying. I'll need those men's names and descriptions now.' Randy who had just gone through this procedure in Cameron Corners rattled off their names, along with descriptions of Van Connely, Trapper and Archie Slater.

'That name — Archie Slater — seems to ring a bell. I think I have an old warrant on him. A killer, if I remember, a hot hand with a gun.'

'Sounds like him. I wouldn't be surprised if you have old warrants on all three of them as well as Burns.'

The marshal finished scribbling notes to himself and then asked, 'What about the other three? Do you know where they're headed?'

'None. No idea at all. That was one of the reasons I came in here — to ask if anyone had seen these men ride out, which direction they would be most likely to take.'

'Temple City would be my guess,' the man in the corner muttered.

'Could be,' Marshal Traylor said thoughtfully. 'There's not much else around west of here. And that's the direction they took unless they were just laying a false trail.'

'I'd start tracking in that direction,' the red-faced man said to Randy. 'You'll likely cut their sign, and if they switched directions, you'll know. If you're any kind of tracker.'

160

'I'm not so sure I am,' Randy admitted.

'What are you thinking, Resolute?' the marshal asked. 'Pardon me, son, I was remiss in not introducing you two. This is Resolute Duncan. Used to be my deputy before the years caught up with him.'

'I resent that, Ben,' Resolute Duncan said, stirring in his chair. 'You know that the town council only used that as an excuse so Bradford's son could take my job.'

Randy could see that the two were going to rehash an old discussion, so he reached for his hat and planted it. 'I've got to be going, men.' This was as close as he had ever been to catching up with Van Connely, and he meant to waste no time.

'Want me to go with you?' Resolute Duncan asked, rising. 'All I need is enough time to throw a saddle on my horse.' He paused and smiled, his thick lips parting slightly. 'Me, I'm one of the best trackers in the territory — isn't that right, Ben?'

'It's right,' the marshal replied without reluctance. 'You know I can't be paying you for any assistance you might give this young man.'

'I didn't ask you to,' Resolute said with a brief display of temper. 'And I wouldn't take spit from the town council. It's just civic duty, and the wish to be doing something. I'm getting fat as a hog now that I'm not working.'

It was still mid-morning when they trailed out of Hazlit, the sun riding high in a crystalline sky. There was a cool, fitful wind blowing, the last remnant of the storm that had passed. Resolute rode an off-white gelding with a gray mane and tail and a few flecks of gray on either side of its rump. For some reason Randy's black didn't seem to like the other animal. Twice he tried to nip its shoulder.

'Bad tempered, ain't he?' Resolute commented after the second attempt.

'He's got a lot of faults,' Randy answered. 'Up till now I was the only one he'd tried to bite.'

Not Kate. That thought shifted and took the form of fond remembrance in his mind. He rode silently beside Resolute as they reached the sun bright creek and crossed it, their horses sending up fans of water, making tiny rainbows in the sun. After riding up the sandy bank on the far side of the creek, Resolute reined in his horse, took off his hat, ran his wrist across his forehead, and swung briefly down.

'Here they go again,' he said, indicating fresh hoof prints. He then only stared at the tracks for a minute or two. 'I've got 'em memorized now,' he said. 'This one long-striding animal has a chip in his left hind shoe. See that?'

Randy didn't, but he was already glad that he had taken on Resolute. He just had never learned the tricks of man-hunting. Resolute had had more than twenty years working the trade. Randy asked as they rode westward, 'Was that true, what you were saying about the town council pensioning you off so that one of them could put his son to work?'

'True,' Resolute said defiantly. 'Or not true — you asked two questions, Randy. I didn't get 'pensioned off.' I don't get no pension. The marshal will get one — he's an elected official, but not a deputy. I got nothing to show for my years of working for the people of Hazlit.'

'That's tough,' Randy sympathized.

'You should say so! All I've got to look forward is joining the old-timers that sit whittling and telling long-ago stories.'

'Aren't you married?' Randy inquired curiously.

'You bet I am!' Resolute said, raising a finger to indicate the direction they should travel across a brushy ravine. 'That's one reason I offered to come along.'

Randy frowned. 'I don't get you,' he said.

'You don't? It's like this, my young friend. A woman might be a good and faithful wife when you've got a job and are out of her hair for most of the day, might cook a fine dinner for you to come home to at night. But ... I sometimes think they let resentment build up over the years, and when you're not doing anything but getting in the way while they're still doing as much work as ever, they seem to get angry easier, start carping at you even though you've done nothing wrong, nothing you could help doing. They seem almost like they're trying to get even for the lean years they've endured — especially when dinner has to be made up of roots and fat meat instead of the plump roasts they used to be able to afford to buy.'

'I see,' was all Randy could think to say.

'I doubt it. I hope you never have to find out,' Resolute said as they crested the canyon rim and continued on westward, Resolute still studying the tracks they were following. The land now was chaparral, dominated by purple sage and much creosote and sumac. Randy could see nothing ahead of them.

'Did you come along with me to try solve things at home?' he asked.

'Sort of — mostly to just get away for a while, but this could be to my advantage, too.'

'In what way?'

'Those boys — at least two of them have reward posters out on them, don't they?'

'I hadn't thought of that.'

'I have,' Resolute said smiling distantly. 'The bank might have a reward up too, by the time we get back. Besides, I mean to show the people of that town that I am still the man for the job. You don't see young Bradford, or the marshal out tracking these bank robbers down, do you? No, sir, I mean to show Hazlit what a washed-up old man can do!'

They rode on mostly in silence after that, Resolute showing the way with certainty, although Randy had to admit he could not always see the tracks the horses of Van Connely's gang had made over the broken, rocky ground. The day remained bright, the wind cool as sunset began to settle and they paused their ponies on a low knoll to peer into the distance toward the scarlet sun which flushed the land.

'There 'tis, son,' Resolute said, drawing in his breath heavily. The long ride had betrayed his protestations of age.

'What?' Randy asked, seeing nothing across the long brush-covered land.

'Dead ahead,' Resolute said proudly, his eyes apparently being sharper than the younger man's. 'That is Temple City right there. And unless our quarry has made a sudden decision to veer off their course, that is where we will find them.'

At dusk they rode the main street of Temple City. Randy was beginning to think that all of these remote border towns had been designed by the same drunken planner. Their sameness was the only thing notable about them.

Overhead a large flight of doves was winging its way homeward as darkness began to settle across the desert. Nobody was about. The good folks of the town were home sitting down to supper and the local no-goods did not emerge from their lairs in the daylight.

'Do you see a hotel?' Randy asked. Resolute pointed up the street.

'That might be a little boarding house. There's a few men standing around.'

'All right. Keep your eyes open.'

'Two horses standing right out front,' Resolute said. 'I'd like a peek at their left hind hoofs.'

'Don't bother,' Randy said as they neared the horses. He had never seen the ponies before that he could remember, but each was branded HF-connected. 'They're here.'

'You sure?'

'I'm sure. How do you want to do this? Ask the local law for help?'

'No!' Resolute said so sharply that Randy looked at him. He could see it in

Resolute's eyes — he was still thinking about the bounty on the heads of the bank robbers, and the red-headed man meant to be given credit for their capture. 'There's a set of outside stairs,' Resolute said. 'How 'bout if I go up that way and you pass through the lobby to see if you can find out what room they're in.'

'All right,' Randy answered. He had no better plan to suggest. So long as they were here and he didn't meet them in the hotel lobby by himself, it seemed that it had a chance of working. He swung down feeling his muscles and stomach tighten oddly. For the first time since this had begun, he was feeling very nervous. But he had come too far, traveled too many hours, days, weeks to give it up now. Tying up the black next to the other HF-connected horses, he stepped up onto the boardwalk and walked past a group of bored, indifferent men and into the hotel.

There were two horses out front.

Only two — that meant that one of them was missing or perhaps tending to his animal, or . . . perhaps anything. Randy crossed the unpolished floor to the counter where a bored woman built like a ball of dough waited.

'I'm looking for someone,' Randy said, and he gave her a sketchy description. 'Those are their horses out front.'

'I recall at least one of them, I think the one with long hair and a smudge of a beard. Kind of distinctive, you know.'

Trapper McGee. Randy's stomach tightened a little more as the clerk checked her book. 'I wasn't here when they checked in — would that have been earlier today? Oh, yeah, here they are. My husband put them in 200 and 202, upstairs.' Randy glanced that way.

'Would that be at that end, or this?'

'Other end,' she told him. Still Randy hesitated, but there was nothing to do now except face the thieves down, and so he started for the inside staircase. Reaching the second-floor landing, he looked up. In the shadows by the outside stairway, Resolute Duncan stood, gun in hand.

Drawing his own Colt, Randy Staggs jabbed a finger at the two doors to his left. Resolute approached him like a cat despite his hard-soled boots. Randy looked at the side-by-side doors and shrugged, cupping his ear. Resolute Duncan nodded and crept to the nearest door to listen. After a minute he shook his head and eased up to the other door. He looked up at Randy, smiled and winked. He had heard something inside the room.

Resolute's hand rested on the knob. Randy saw that there was no lock on the door. He took a deep, calming breath and watched as Resolute turned the brass knob. When the latch slid back Resolute flung the door wide. Randy Staggs had a glimpse of Trapper McGee sitting on a bed, pulling his boot on. Archie Slater was at a mirror, shaving, his back turned toward them. Both men moved with the amazing speed ingrained in those who had lived long on the dangerous edge of survival.

Trapper threw his boot at Randy who ducked it and rolled on the bed to grab for his gun. Before Randy could react there were two quick shots. Trapper's bullet missed Randy by inches and plowed its way into the wall of the room. Resolute's answering shot might have been slower, but it was better aimed.

His bullet tagged Trapper on the chin exactly on that thumbprint of a beard he wore, and blew his face apart, severing his spinal column as it exited. Archie Slater had been moving at the same time. He had a gun in his hand, but he changed his mind as he faced the two armed men in front of him, leaped toward the window and through it to tumble onto the alley below. Randy took a shot at him, but it went wild as Slater rose and limped off up the alley. Randy shouted a meaningless warning after

Slater, and ran toward the outside stairs.

He reached the street in time to see Slater swing onto his horse and heel it sharply as the men who had been gathered in a knot there now fled in a confused dash toward safety. Before Randy could react, the big-chested sorrel horse Slater was riding was nearly at full speed, charging down at him. Randy ducked instinctively, rolled and reached out reflexively. He managed to catch hold of Slater's left stirrup. The jolt to his shoulders nearly caused him to black out, but he clung to his trophy knowing that he might never get this close to his quarry again.

Slater howled out a savage warning with no articulate words in it, slipped his boot from the stirrup and kicked wildly at Randy's clinging hands as his horse drove the length of the main street. Randy pawed at the foot, finally caught it by the ankle with one hand and then released his grip on the stirrup to clench his other hand around Slater's foot.

They raced on another fifty yards, Randy gripping Slater's boot desperately until Slater turned in the saddle and drew his gun, trying to beat Randy away or to shoot him — which he had in mind made no difference, for all he accomplished was losing the reins, and with one foot only in the stirrups to hold him in the saddle, he was yanked from his perch.

Slater and Randy went rolling in the dust. Slater took the worst of it, falling from height. They both flipped over as the panicked sorrel pounded on. Randy could hear the breath expelled violently from Archie Slater's chest, and he thought the man was done. But a split second later, Slater was seated in the dust, his revolver clenched tightly in both hands. Randy heard him snarl:

'I never did like you, Staggs.'

There was no other way to do it; Randy shot him where he knelt and Slater toppled over, his gun unfired.

Rising shakily, Randy dusted himself off as a crowd of men raced up the street toward him, a panting Resolute Duncan at their head. Randy staggered toward Resolute as onlookers discussed and debated among themselves and hovered curiously over the dead form of Archie Slater.

'I guess now,' Randy said, clinging to Resolute, 'we'd better have a talk with the local law.'

9

They never did find Van Connely, despite their searching. No one had seen him since the three outlaws had ridden into town. It didn't matter much just then, Randy considered. If Connely had witnessed any of what had happened, he would be long gone out onto the desert, hoping to avoid capture. The town marshal of Temple City knew Resolute Duncan and readily accepted his version of the events. The stolen bank loot was easily found under one of the hotel room beds.

They left Temple City in the middle of the afternoon, hoping to reach Hazlit before nightfall. It seemed unlikely they would make it in the hours remaining, but they both wanted to return as quickly as possible. For Randy's part, if it were humanly possible he would have ridden all night and all of the following days without a pause for rest. He wanted, needed to get back to the Lynch Ranch. His imagination filled with images of Kate waiting to greet him in the door.

With the purple light of dusk spreading across the land, Resolute Duncan lifted his arm toward a low knoll where three oak trees stood, two of them black and lifeless as the result of an old fire. 'We're going to have to rest, Randy. This looks like as good a place as we're likely to find before dark.'

Randy glanced toward the knoll and nodded, turning the head of his black horse in that direction. He swung down and loosened the cinches of his saddle. The wind was rising again with the sun sinking in the west and the horse's mane and tail drifted as it blew. Looking around, Randy saw there was little forage: only a clump or two of buffalo grass and some patches of wild oats.

'You'll have to make out the best you

can,' he told the horse. Lugging his saddle, he sat down on the ground beside the trunk of the living oak tree and watched as Resolute fussed with his saddlebags. Randy noticed that he had not removed the saddle from the white and gray gelding.

'Lose something?' Randy asked from the ground where he rested, legs crossed, arms wrapped around his drawn-up knees.

'No,' the red-haired man said with a lopsided smile. His movements seemed tentative as he strode up to where Randy sat. His hand was on the butt of his revolver, and as he reached Randy, he drew it.

'I'll have to ask you to shed that Colt of yours,' Resolute said.

'What . . . what in hell are you planning on doing?' Randy asked, but he removed his pistol from its holster and handed it to Resolute. The former deputy now had a look in his eyes that seemed to say he meant business.

'What am I doing?' Resolute said

with a harsh laugh. 'Poking the town of Hazlit in the eye.'

'You mean you're taking the bank's money,' Randy said.

'That's exactly what I mean,' Resolute said roughly.

'But, Resolute . . . it's not worth it! You'll have money soon. There's the reward for Trapper McGee — I'll tell the marshal that you got him. There's that and a reward from the bank for bringing their money back.'

'You assume a lot,' Resolute said, standing over Randy, his cocked pistol in his hand. He was only a bulky, menacing silhouette before the sundown sky now. 'I never saw no poster on Trapper McGee — did you?'

'No, but — '

'And as for the bank offering a reward for the stolen money, it wouldn't be much. You can bet on that. I'd be lucky if I got enough to survive the month. No, Randy, I'll take what I have and ride as far away from that town as I can.' Anger now surged in his voice as he considered past real or imagined slights from the town. 'I don't need their handouts.'

'Resolute,' Randy coaxed, trying to keep his voice even, 'you've lived a long time on the right side of the law. Don't give it up now. Besides,' he added, 'you've got a wife back in Hazlit, think of what this will do to her.'

'I really don't care what happens to Ella. Weren't you listening to what I told you along the trail, Randy, I hate that woman!'

There seemed to be nothing else to say. He spread his hands in a pleading gesture just as Resolute slammed the barrel of his pistol against the side of Randy's head. Randy pitched forward and lay sprawled against the earth, tasting blood in his mouth. He couldn't have gotten up if he had wished to. He only lay there, listening to the saddle leather creak as Resolute Duncan lifted himself into it, the steady clopping of his horse's hoofs as it was ridden eastward.

Slowly Randy hoisted himself to his feet, his head reeling. He staggered like a drunken man to where he had dropped his saddle and pulled his long gun from its scabbard. Resolute was far gone now. Randy could see him a hundred yards away, his horse at a canter. Randy rested his left hand against the trunk of the oak tree and spread his thumb to form a rest for his rifle barrel.

He squinted through the sights of the Winchester, aiming the front bead to allow for drop and windage. Then slowly he pulled the trigger and watched. And waited. It seemed like a full minute before he saw a reaction from Resolute. The former deputy jerked upright in the saddle, slapped futilely at his back and then slipped from the saddle to lie dead against the cold earth. The black horse, which had been startled by the shot, turned and fixed an evil stare on Randy as he gathered up his saddle and walked towards him.

'I couldn't just let him get away with it, could I?' he muttered to the black.

In truth Randy Staggs felt neither pride in his marksmanship nor sorrow over the death of Resolute Duncan. It was with an oddly detached sense of being that he rode to where Resolute lay, collected the reins to the white horse and made camp not far away from where the desperate deputy rested. In the morning, Randy was thinking, he would be feeling stronger, his head would be clearer and he would tie Resolute across his saddle and return him to Hazlit town to be buried.

Randy slept long but not restfully. His head had continued to throb unmercifully through the night for one thing. For another, he had some explaining to do in Hazlit. And then there was Kate — far away. Was she waiting for him? Had he made too much of her casual kindness.

The morning sun was welcome, and Randy rose from the dewy grass and started on his way, leading Resolute's horse with its unhappy burden. His mind worked again on what he was going to say as Hazlit appeared on the distant horizon. There was no point in darkening the dead man's reputation now that he was gone. Randy decided with a mental sigh that he would simply tell a few uncomplicated lies. These could do no harm to anyone. They might even do some good if Hazlit started to develop a conscience about the way it treated the men it had formerly employed.

At 2 p.m. he reined the black up in front of Marshal Ben Traylor's office and swung stiffly from the saddle. A few townspeople had gathered at the sight of the dead man, recognizing the white horse, but Randy paid them no mind as he unstrapped the saddle-bags containing the bank's money and trudged up across the plankwalk into the marshal's office.

Traylor was not there, a young bright-eyed man wearing a shield told him. Randy took him to be Bradford, the kid who had supplanted Resolute Duncan as deputy marshal.

'I'll just wait,' Randy said and the young man nodded, eyeing the trail-dusty, battered visitor with saddle-bags on his shoulder, a gun on his hip. Randy sat in the farthest chair from the marshal's desk, only now realizing how he must appear. He had been pistol-whipped and trampled over, and though he had no mirror to confirm it, his face must have shown some bruising. He couldn't remember the last time he had bathed or shaved, and he must have smelled strongly of horse. All of that was unimportant; this was no beauty contest. He needed to talk to Traylor.

The marshal stumped in half an hour later, not totally surprised to find Randy Staggs waiting there — he had recognized the two horses at the hitch rail. He only nodded at Randy and told his deputy: 'You'd better start checking the saloons. It's early, but I hear rumblings of trouble out there.'

Traylor sat heavily in his chair and tilted back, his eyes nearly closed. 'Well then, Staggs,' the lawman said, 'I expect you have a story to tell me.'

Randy told him, lying about only half the time. There was no one to dispute his version of events. 'Resolute took out Trapper McGee and Archie Slater, but someone was laying for us along the trail, maybe wanting the bank money. That's when Resolute caught lead. By the way, did you receive any word on whether or not there were bounties posted on any of those men?'

'I'm still waiting for responses to my inquiries,' Traylor said, his eyes narrowing with suspicion.

'If there were bounties, all of the money is to be paid to Resolute — to his widow, that is. I can vouch for Resolute having taken them. I'll write it out if you like.'

'All right.' Traylor who had briefly wondered about Randy's motives in asking, relaxed slightly. Perhaps he had thought Staggs had killed Resolute to help his own chances at earning the rewards.

'As for the bank money,' Randy said, toeing the saddle-bags he had placed at his feet. 'Any reward for that should go to Mrs Duncan too. She deserves to get something from her husband's efforts.'

'Knowing that bank, they'll probably cut a medal out of a tin can and present it to the widow,' Traylor muttered. 'But I'll do what I can. I worked a lot of years with Resolute, and he never did let me down. I'll try to do the same for him.' He rose and so did Randy Staggs. 'You aren't asking for anything for your troubles,' the marshal commented as he walked Randy to the door.

'No. With me it was all about bringing those men down, not about the money. You'll see to Resolute's body and to his horse?' Randy asked as they stepped out into the bright sunlight.

'I'll see that it's all taken care of,' Ben Traylor said, 'and that Mrs Duncan gets whatever's coming to her. What are you going to do?' he asked Randy.

'Sleep. Eat and sleep, then I'll be gone from Hazlit. Not that it's not a nice enough place, but I doubt you'll be seeing me again.'

Taking the black horse's leads, he walked along the dusty street toward the sadly sagging little hotel.

* * *

Morning brought a clear, cool dawn and Randy rode into the face of the rising sun. The black horse moved easily and eagerly beneath him as if it knew the direction they were now traveling and wanted to reach the Pocono. Randy was every bit as eager. He regretted having to stop and camp out that night when they stopped not far south of Cameron Corners. He could have reached the town easily, but he had little money left — all in small silver coins, and he was in no hurry to ever see Cameron Corners or any of the small desert towns again. He slept long but uncomfortably, and was up again with the first light of the following dawn.

He continued to strain his eyes, searching the far horizon — a futile exercise since he was still many miles from the Pocono country and the possible salvation it offered.

The day grew warmer than the past few had been. He wove his way through the acre-sized stands of nopal cactus, sage, laurel-leaf sumac and twisted manzanita. The land was rocky again, and some of the slopes were treacherous beneath the black's hoofs, but they continued on their way doggedly, pausing only at the occasional ponds or winding rivulets they found for water.

He was still not familiar with the land, but at sundown on this evening he thought he was beginning to recognize certain landmarks, and believed that they could reach the Pocono the following day. With that comforting thought in his mind, he again lay his battered body down to sleep in the faraway country where no hellrakers roamed to disturb the silence of the night.

* * *

The Lynch ranch appeared almost magically from between its enclosing hills and Randy Staggs drew up his black horse to sit looking down at it. For a moment he felt a twinge of anxiety surge through his thoughts. What if Kate was gone? She might have found that she did not have the funds and the determination to continue working the enterprise, having no real hope for a future with the horse herd lost.

As far as that went, he reflected, what was he bringing back to Kate? No treasure, no hope or promise for a better future. Just his ragged self and a worn-out black horse. He started down the hill toward the ranch.

10

She emerged from the stone house into the brilliant sunlight of late afternoon, raised her aproned skirt and began waving wildly. Randy had trouble holding the black horse back. They were coming home! Or as close to a home as either of them had ever had. The welcoming girl moved out into the yard, still waving, her bright smile showing, her eyes, a little damp, gleaming as they approached.

Swinging down, Randy waited. For what? And then he knew, as the girl rushed into his arms, crying deeply now. 'I didn't think you'd make it back,' she said with her face pressed against his shoulder. 'I was almost ready to give up. I'm glad I didn't.' She smiled through the tears as she drew away from him.

The black horse found a way to slip

its head in between them and it began nuzzling Kate insistently. She stroked its muzzle, patted its neck and said, 'Yes you big rascal, I missed you too.'

'I'll unsaddle and see that he's put in with the other two,' Randy said, glancing toward the horse pen. There was only one animal there, the stubby buckskin. Kate flushed a little with shame and said,

'I had to sell the roan. Things were getting that tight. I owed so much . . . '

'It'll be all right,' Randy said, stroking her smooth dark hair. 'Is there anything around that you could make me a meal out of?'

'I'll throw something together,' Kate promised. With a weakening smile she turned and went into the house.

'Come on, you old devil,' Randy said to the black. 'Let's get you settled down.'

Over coffee, after dinner, Randy and Kate sat looking at each other across the table. She said, 'Are you going to tell me about it, Randy?'

191

'One of these days,' he promised. 'It's too near right now. Let me have time to think and I'll tell you all about it, after I make up a few stories of my bravery.'

They sat up late by the fire. Kate did most of the talking, and much of what she said was saddening. Her debts and those her father had left behind when he took his fateful journey, had eaten up the gold that Randy had delivered to her. How she was going to eke out another year's existence on the land was unimaginable. There was nothing Randy could say or think of doing. He would be willing to work for her day and night, but rangeland without stock was only useless property.

If he could have thought of a way to save the herd for her . . . but it was long gone by now. As he lay awake in Skyler Lynch's bed that night, Randy was unable to go to sleep despite his weariness. Looking back, he should have waited a few days more and seen if the bank was going to come up with a decent reward, if there were bounties to be paid on the heads of Trapper McGee and Archie Slater, enough that he could have shared some of it with Mrs Duncan and still had enough to lighten Kate's heavy load. But he had been too rash, in too much of a hurry to return to her.

And he had arrived empty-handed, no white knight, only an extra burden. Twice as many people to feed, twice the number of horses to provide for. Despite his high hopes and good intentions he had returned simply as a broken down saddle tramp.

'Sorry, Captain,' he muttered once before he rolled over, put his face on the pillow and willed himself to sleep.

* * *

Morning was bright and clear again. He could hear Kate singing softly in the kitchen as she boiled coffee for them. Randy went out into the glare of the sun-bright day to see to the horses. As he crossed the yard, the shaggy buckskin lifted its head and ambled over to greet him at the gate. The black, predictably, backed away into a far corner. It did not wish to be ridden on this morning. Randy muttered a curse in its direction and stroked the buckskin's muzzle.

They had plenty of water, it seemed, but only a few wisps of hay. He would find the hay wagon and bring their fodder to them, if hay there was. If not he would take them from the pen and stake them out on the best graze he could find.

He sensed an approaching rider's presence before he either saw or heard him. The visitor rode a gray horse through the scattered oaks, approaching the house. Randy released the buckskin's head and went out to meet the incoming man. He could not see his face; his tugged-down Stetson cast a deep shadow across it.

Randy stood watching, hands on his hips. There was something familiar about the man, but . . . '

By the time he recognized Van Connely, he had already drawn his gun and held it steadily leveled at Randy as he swung down from the gray horse and walked toward him, his eyes darting this way and that.

'There anybody else around?' Van Connely asked.

'No,' Randy lied. He wanted to keep Kate well clear of this — whatever it proved to be. 'What are you doing here, Connely? How did you even find me?'

'Finding you wasn't difficult,' Van Connely answered. 'Everyone working for Skyler Lynch knew he was driving the herd this way, that he had a ranch here. Once I got into the Pocono country, it was only a matter of asking around.'

'Why are you here?' Randy asked uneasily, his eyes fixed on the shiny Colt revolver in Van Connely's hand. 'I've got nothing you could want.'

'No, but you took something I needed,' Connely said, stepping even nearer. 'My whole damned gang! And you would have taken me out, too, if I hadn't happened to slip out for a game of chance.'

'Those men weren't friends of yours,' Randy tried. Van Connely's eyes remained fixed on him now. He smiled distantly.

'Not in any real sense, I'll grant you. But I could trust them to do what I wanted. I got along well enough with Trapper and Archie Slater, even Shawnee Burns, stupid drunk that he was. The point is, I was able to work with them. None of them would have ever crossed me. We were just starting to make money — you ruined that, Staggs. You left me wandering around like a one-legged man with no one there to prop me up. The jobs I had planned well, I just had to abandon them. There's that . . . and the money!'

'You stole four thousand dollars from me, Staggs,' Van Connely said vehemently.

'I never knew how much it was,' Randy said. 'Besides, most people would say that the money belonged to the bank and to the people who had deposited it there, not to you.'

'No matter — I had it in my hands; that made it mine. What did you do with it? Don't tell me that it was something heroic like returning it to the bank?'

'That's it,' Randy admitted. He could see that Connely didn't believe him.

'Even you can't be that stupid,' Connely said, growing more menacing. 'Where is it?'

'I told you that I don't have it.'

'I hope you do, Staggs,' Van Connely said, 'otherwise I'll just have to shoot you down for the inconvenience you've caused me, making me ride all the way back here.'

Randy couldn't understand Van Connely's logic, but he knew that the man was serious. He was determined to be paid back one way or the other.

To his left Randy heard a sound and he glanced that way to see Kate Lynch standing on the porch, fingertips to her lips. Van looked that way as well. 'Get over here, girl!' he ordered. Then to Randy he said, 'You told me there was no one else here.'

'I meant no one with a gun. That's the captain's daughter, Connely. Leave her alone.'

'I will,' Van Connely said, smiling, 'or I won't. Does she know where the money is?'

'She knows it's back in the bank.'

Connely didn't like that answer. 'Get over here closer, girl,' he commanded and Kate inched uncertainly nearer. Her eyes, when they met Randy's were filled with worry and pain. Van Connely's manner was no longer bland. There was a slow anger building in him, and Randy could see it. If he had taken the time to strap his gun on this morning, he would have taken his chance to stop Connely no matter the outcome. But he stood there naked as a baby, his handgun on the bedpost in the captains' room.

'I was hoping you would make this

easier on me, Staggs,' Connely said, taking one step nearer as he cocked his pistol. 'I don't need you — the girl will help me search the place. And if she knows anything, believe me, I'll find out.'

He raised his pistol then, but he was too slow.

There was a rush of dark impulse like storm clouds suddenly shuttering the sun, a heavy pounding and as Connely looked toward the rearing menace, he was already too late. The black horse reared high and now drove its front hoofs down with mallet-like precision, a thousand pounds of muscle behind them and Connely went down in a puff of dust like a sack of grain. The black horse reared up again, settled and snorted and walked away.

'My God!' Kate said in a soft whisper. Then she walked past the battered form of Van Connely without glancing at him and threw her arms around Randy's waist, clinging to him.

'That black devil,' Randy said. 'He's

a dangerous beast.'

'Randy!' Kate said, leaning her head back so that he could look down at her face. 'He saved your life.'

'Only by chance.'

'No, not by chance. That horse is your friend, Randy. He knew you needed help and he came to aid you!'

'You're being silly now,' Randy said. Kate was trembling in his arms, and he found himself shaking a little. Despite his words, Randy looked toward the corral where the black horse poked around at the last wisps of hay in the feed trough, and he wondered. No, he told himself sharply, the horse was a temperamental beast with a nasty temper. It was a wonder it hadn't trampled Randy himself somewhere along the way.

'Let me take you inside,' Randy said to Kate, brushing back a strand of her shining dark hair.

'No,' she protested. 'I'd rather go alone. I have to pull myself together.'

'All right. I guess I'd better see to

. . . that,' he said, gesturing vaguely toward Van Connely's ravaged body. As he walked toward him he watched the two horses in the pen. He hadn't noticed before, had no need to observe, but the shaggy, stocky buckskin horse Kate had kept was a mare — and his black was paying it an unusual amount of attention. Possibly, Randy thought fleetingly, that was why the black had attacked. Trying to protect a potential mate.

If they ever were to breed, that would be a mix! A bunch of stubby, hairy, mule-headed colts with the evil temper of their father. Of course Kate, optimist that she was, would suggest that it could go the other way — a breed of tall, sleek, gentle black horses. All of which speculation was unimportant at the moment. The gray horse Van Connely had ridden stood nearby, reins hanging, looking like an uncertain interloper at a party.

Crouching down, Randy kept his eyes averted from Van Connely's crushed skull, but he searched through the gambler's pockets. He found a purse containing nearly four hundred dollars — Van's luck at the gambling tables must have finally turned. Also in an inside coat pocket he found a much-folded wanted poster for Van Connely, advertising a thousand-dollar reward. The bandit must have kept it out of vanity. Randy tucked it away in his own pocket along with the cash.

Connely could be placed in the back of the hay wagon and drawn to the nearest town where the reward could be applied for. Randy knew how long these things took to be verified and paid, but perhaps one day they would receive enough to keep the ranch afloat until they could become productive again.

It was all vague hopes and uncertain planning, but it gave Randy a sense that perhaps his own luck was turning — and Kate's. Rising, he found that he was still shaky. He went to the gray horse, unsaddled it and slipped its bit. He thought that the sight of the strange horse might set the black off again, but his horse was still too distracted by the mare to pay it any attention. To be on the safe side, Randy took the gray to the barn and settled it in with feed and water before he returned to the house to talk to Kate.

He found her at the kitchen table, studying an empty coffee cup while she propped up her head with her small hands, which somehow gave the impression of weariness.

'Is it done?' she asked.

'Not yet. I'm going to have to use the wagon to take him into town.' He then unfolded the reward poster in front of her and placed the money he had found beside it on the old plank table. 'It might be a good idea if you went along to help me explain things — you're well known around here; I'm not.'

'All right,' Kate said heavily. 'Can they give a reward to a horse?' she asked with a flickering smile.

'Who knows!' Randy laughed. 'With

the way you feel about the devil, you can convince them, like you've half-convinced me, that he was trained well enough, faithful enough to rush forward to aid us at your signal.'

'I can try it,' Kate said, her smile growing larger. 'What about this?' she asked, fingering the stack of money that had been concealed in Van Connely's purse. 'Is it stolen, too?'

'Somehow, I don't think so. Van always thought of himself as a gambler first and foremost. It looks as if he finally had a good run of cards. All the judges in this territory, Solomon himself, could never discover where the money came from or who might have a claim to it. I say we just tuck it away and keep the ranch going as best we can until our new crop of horses starts coming in.'

Kate looked at him questioningly and he explained about the black's interest in the shaggy buckskin mare.

'It's a good thing I kept her and sold the roan gelding then,' she laughed and Randy smiled. The room seemed suddenly cozier, warmer. More like a home.

'We'll make it, Kate,' he said, taking her small hand in his work-roughened grip. 'I don't know exactly how yet, but everyone's life is a series of everyday problems that have to be solved again and again. Most everybody does make it through somehow.'

He paused and looked away through the sunlit window. 'I'll feel guilty for a long while about not being able to save the horse herd. All I brought you was the black devil and one wandering, raggedy man. It seems that I let you down, that I lost your future out there on the trail.'

'It seems to me,' Kate said, rising to look out of the window with her hands clasped behind her back, 'that you have done a very good job of bringing my future to me, Mr Staggs.'

When she turned back to face him she was smiling, and Randy decided that no matter what he had done or failed to do, she had brought a promising future to him.

In the corral the black stallion was whinnying triumphantly.

THE END

We do hope that you have enjoyed reading this large print book.

Did you know that all of our titles are available for purchase?

We publish a wide range of high quality large print books including:
Romances, Mysteries, Classics
General Fiction
Non Fiction and Westerns

Special interest titles available in large print are:
The Little Oxford Dictionary
Music Book, Song Book
Hymn Book, Service Book

Also available from us courtesy of Oxford University Press:
Young Readers' Dictionary
(large print edition)
Young Readers' Thesaurus
(large print edition)

For further information or a free brochure, please contact us at:
Ulverscroft Large Print Books Ltd.,
The Green, Bradgate Road, Anstey,
Leicester, LE7 7FU, England.
Tel: (00 44) 0116 236 4325
Fax: (00 44) 0116 234 0205

THE DEVIL'S PAYROLL

Paul Green

When bounty hunter John Harrison captures fugitive outlaw Clay Barton, he's persuaded by Maggie Sloane to allow the captive to lead them to the loot robbed from an army payroll. But Barton double-crosses them and the mysterious Leo Gabriel kidnaps Maggie. With a veteran Buffalo Soldier, Sergeant Eli Johnson, at his side, Harrison battles ruthless vaqueros and a Comanche war party to recover the money, re-capture Barton and rescue Maggie . . . but a surprise awaits him when he finally catches up with his enemies . . .

HELL ON HOOFS

Lance Howard

Arriving in Lancerville, John Laramie hoped to escape his old life as a man-hunter and settle down. But there he finds he's torn between the demons of his past and hope for a brighter future when a young woman seeks his help in getting rid of a vicious outlaw. Then the Cross Gang attacks him and the young woman's life is put in danger. But will it cost Laramie more to win than to lose in a deadly showdown?